KALIVAS!

Cover by Joel Amat Güell

ISBN: 9781960988799 (paperback)

CLASH Books
Troy, NY
clashbooks.com
Distributed by Consortium

First Edition 2025
Printed in the United States of America.

Praise for Nick Mamatas

"An inventive, invigorating science fiction romp. This is the nanobot Shakespeare our dystopian lives demand."

— Silvia Moreno-Garcia, author of *Mexican Gothic*

"Dripping with slippery decadence, dark humor, and drones, *Kalivas!* is the version of Shakespeare we need as an antidote to the ascendency of the tech bros. Like what might happen if you crossed Gene Wolfe with William Gibson, forced the resulting hybrid to sit in a series of tech product launches, and asked it to predict the future." "

— Brian Evenson, author of *Last Days*

"*Kalivas!* is not only a hilariously self-aware reworking of *The Tempest* but a vertiginously deep dive into the monstrous id of the techno-oligarchs of our own day, and the catastrophic futures they would call their dreams." "

— Vajra Chandrasekera, author of *The Saint of Bright Doors* and *Rakesfall*

"“Mamatas is the People's Commissar of Awesome.”

— CHINA MIÉVILLE, AUTHOR OF *EMBASSYTOWN*

Mamatas's bold, masterful voice comes through once again, in notes both harsh and heartbreaking, making us see familiar things strangely and strange things as intimately relatable as our own skin. Anyone not reading his work is only hurting themselves."

— CATHERYNNE M. VALENTE, AUTHOR OF *SPACE OPERA* AND THE *FAIRYLAND* SERIES

A sci-fi novel of ideas, part game theory, part theater, *Kalivas!* is deep, funny, and wild. From its reversals of fortune to its grand completion, it is a song of resistance to the absurd notion that some are meant to rule while others meant to serve."

— VANESSA VASELKA, AUTHOR OF *ZAZEN* AND *THE GREAT OFFSHORE GROUNDS*

Kalivas!

Or, Another Tempest

Nick Mamatas

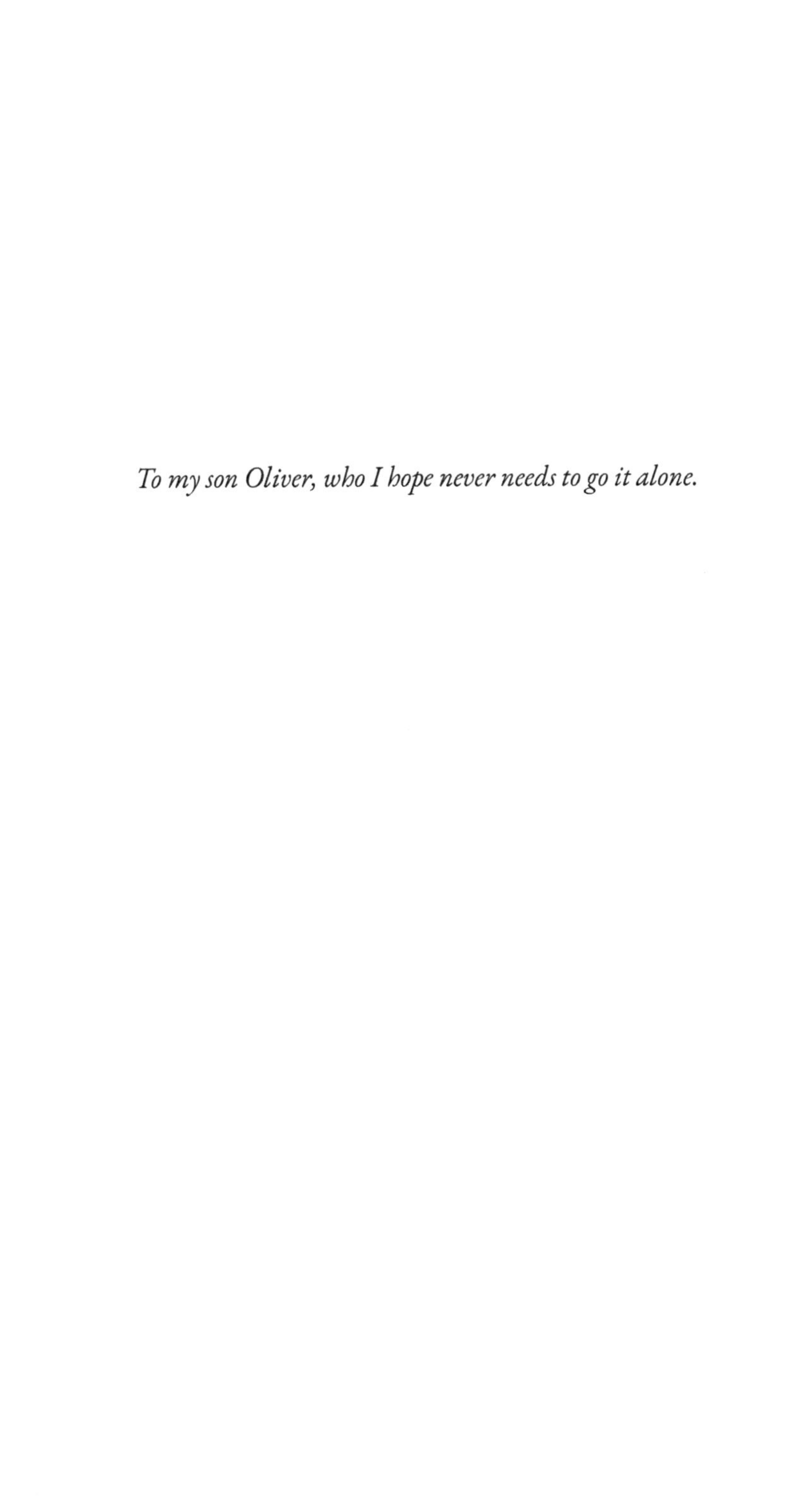

To my son Oliver, who I hope never needs to go it alone.

1

The Master doesn't make it rain much anymore, except for when he lets me fish and provides a drizzle to lure my little prey up to the surface of the water. Even the Master can't keep it from raining naturally though, and so it was raining hard, and inconveniently, and I waited out the lightning storm under a tree, which was a foolish thing to do. I could have died, but the path down to the island's cliff face was washing away, so I could have died trying to run for home too.

The storm smelled of nature rather than magic, anyway. Like salt and burning steel. It hadn't arrived on Master's schedule, and it was a big one. The rain, and lightning and thunder, especially unusual in the Bay Area, lasted a day and a night. I don't sleep much anyway. Too busy being alive.

When I was young, my mother told me a story of when she was young and had first moved to California from Boston, where she had completed her degree. Cambridge, actually, but she always said Boston. She didn't have a car, didn't need one, couldn't drive, which is why she moved here instead of anywhere else when she had to leave Boston with an attaché case full of her notebooks and her very tiny inventions. Lots of trains and buses she could take instead of investing in a car or hailing one from her phone, and she occasionally rode a bicycle or scooter. It was on an early bus trip up into the hills to see her PhD advisor that it started raining, thundering. Lighting! And the people on the bus with her, mostly older people, or street people who couldn't afford to hail a car or own one, shook in fear, and one older man even cried out to his Lord and Savior Jesus Christ for help.

And my mother explained to me, these people all grew up and lived every day with the knowledge that they dwelled atop the Hayward fault, which one day certainly would destroy them all, but they were afraid of thunder because it was unusual.

The morning after that bus trip and an eventful evening with her advisor, the fault did generate another quake. A big one, as large as the M 6.8 of 1868. Then there were aftershocks. Then another giant quake a week later, and another. A trillion dollars vanished into fissures and the pockets of politicians. The hills came down. The forests turned to ash. Everything changed. That's why she remembered the bus trip. My mother was two hundred years old when she first told me of her bus trip, of how it's the usual and expected that'll likely kill you, not the fearsome and strange.

Which is why, when the storm let up finally, I ventured down toward the cliff and peered across the water to Saddle Rock, where a boat had smashed up. A few waterlogged bodies were floating atop the swells. Maybe the sharks would get 'em, which would be a thing to see, but more likely they'd be buffet rafts for seabirds.

Then came M, perfectly dry, all in white without a

speck of mud on either her clothes or her skin. M means many things. The Master's daughter is one. And another is Mira!

"Mira, Mister Kalivas!" she said, more to herself than to me, though she honored me with a glance as she walked past me to the very edge of the cliff I was squatting near. She had more than perfect vision, M did, more than perfect everything. Her freckles she wore because she wanted them. A scattering across the arms and cheeks today. Red curls like the copper springs from an ancient machine my mother would have known something about, and so unlike her father's Latin features and dark skin.

"Kita," I said to her, pointing out the bodies. She'd been looking at the wreckage of the ship.

"Silly, nobody speaks Greek anymore," she told me.

"Nobody around here speaks Spanish, except for you."

"I like to honor this place." Her father, she seemed to feel, did not. The Master was in exile here, so who could blame him. But he was in exile from San Francisco and lamented it often, but he called it Saint Francis, to be annoying.

And he called me "hut-dweller," to be annoying. And also accurate.

"Are they human?" I asked M of the bodies.

"Of course they are," she said. "They're wearing clothes. They used tools...albeit not well." She laughed, a big snort on a little thing, and gestured toward the shattered rock.

"Storm must have done it," I said.

"You're a genius, Mister Kalivas."

"I mean, if they weren't human, they would have known the storm was coming and stayed home. They would have turned back, or grown gills and jumped overboard for fun. The weather caught them by surprise, like weather does to a human."

"Sorry," M said. "I hope you don't catch pneumonia and die. I'd miss you."

"I'd miss you too, Miss, but the unusual and unexpected isn't what kills."

"What?!" She turned her head to me, brown eyes burning.

"Just something that occurred to me," I said. Neither the Master nor M liked it much when I was able to lead a conversation down a pathway they hadn't considered.

"You don't know what you're talking about. Why do I even deign to speak to you? I don't know. You're wrong. People die in expected ways all the time. Look at these people. Do you think this was some sort of mass suicide—party yacht onto Los Farallones?" M willed away her blush. It was like a switch being thrown.

"Oh," she said.

The birds wheeled into sight and descended onto the bodies.

2

My hut is pretty nice. It's a geodesic dome, with a screen full of games and pornographies and databases, a central fireplace, a watermaker that smells of ozone, and a mattress I could practically sail back to the mainland on if I wanted to, and if I had a sheet worthy of a sail. I've got a sturdy hoop house for growing vegetables right outside, a smokehouse and big freezer for mostly fish and the occasional seal, and a hot tub I don't use much because the islands are very windy. The place vacuums itself, and with a hair dryer I can affect basic repairs. Melt and reshape. These are all products greatly improved upon by my mother's ingenuity, nay, technological wizardry! She enjoyed telling me she was a wizard when the papers by turns lauded and castigated her as a witch, with a cauldron full of nanotech into which you could dip practically anything you wished to improve.

Anything but people, so for my own repairs, I'm not so lucky. I've got some salves from the Master for my skin, and an implant that chugs along whipping up antibodies as needed, and a shrinking supply of extremely large nutrient pills, but that's it.

I hadn't even caught anything before the storm came up, and if I ate anything from the local waters for the next couple of days it would probably taste of gasoline, fiberglass, and men. No flesh for me. Ah well, it's always Lent somewhere.

That's a joke. I know how calendars work.

Yes, I get defensive over castigating myself over jokes I tell myself. When the only beings you know and get to speak with are nigh omniscient, you have to watch every rhetorical step.

It's also always winter and thus always almost but never quite Christmas, so I was glad of my hut, which got one whiff of what I'd been through overnight and warmed right up, spritzed the air with calming aromas, and played violins, a viola, a cello for me.

But all of this is nothing compared to the lighthouse, the abode of the Master and of little M.

Their coming was preceded by a shimmering in the air. Then a glider sailed over. An impressive feat made possible only because for several long moments, the air stilled and grew cold. I own a few firearms, keep them clean, and once in a while fire them pointlessly at the passing peduncle and flukes of a whale, but I approached the glider without weapons. An older man disembarked, with a silent babe in his arms. That was a better trick than piloting a glider.

"These are my islands," I told the old man. At the time, I had a boat I'd occasionally use to visit the smaller ones and collect eggs. Then, in an instant, I didn't. It sank beneath the waves as if pulled from below.

I had all these islands, even the rocks that are named

only in Spanish, and then I didn't. They belonged to the Master now, as did I.

He thanked me for my hospitality and told me to prepare the lighthouse for a child. I was pleased he didn't have designs on my hut.

It took weeks of work. "It's not all my doing, you know," the Master told me, "and not at all my choice," as he watched me scrape bird shit from the windows of the lantern room. His tone was apologetic, but he was mostly addressing M, secondarily himself, and perhaps someone else on a tertiary level. But I was in fourth place somehow, and was part of the conversation, despite being outside, on the catwalk, while he sat in a chair in the middle of the room where, once upon a time, a great Fresnel lens used to be. The baby couldn't talk yet, and the other being the Master often muttered to was and remains nearly entirely unperceivable to me.

"If you had your choice, Master, if you had free will, what would you be doing now? Where would you be?"

"Where I was, of course! The mainland. Society, civilization!"

"Thirty-two miles thataway," I said, hiking my thumb in the direction of the continent. I'd seen the gesture in cartoons. Perhaps one day, an elephant seal will be uplifted and know what the gesture means and offer me a ride to the remains of the wharf.

"Were you born there, or here?"

"There."

"I knew your mother. She was an amazing mind."

"Hmm," I said. I did not want to hear of my mother, not from the mouth of the Master.

The Master looked off into the distance, reading something on the inside of his eyes. "You do good work."

"It would go faster with an extra pair of hands or, you

know, anything." I waggled my fingers at him. I am a cheeky slave, always testing the boundaries, always trying to determine how long the leash is.

"I must conserve my resources," the Master said. "But I have resources sufficient to make life difficult for you."

"Just not sufficient to make it any easier, eh?"

"I can make it shorter," said the Master.

And that was pretty much our relationship. Chores, chatting, chastisement.

And child-rearing. The Master fed M, and played with her, and educated her—the last mostly as she slept in the evenings. But even he knew that his technology was not enough, and that for anyone to be raised properly, they need a second adult of some sort, if only to measure their parent against, in order to properly rise up, overthrow their father, and become an adult in their own right. After I prepared the lighthouse, the Master dismantled the glider and repurposed its mechanisms for other things. It didn't depend on wind after all, but by some sort of electrostatic energy that had been provided by the mainland, and then turned off. The only juice the Master had was from whatever had been injected into his bone marrow in the womb, and whatever his baby could provide to him, which wasn't much, so clearly she needed to grow up, and fast. Big white arms, thick milky thighs. A delicious girl. And I, her new uncle, to replace the evil old one left behind in Saint Francis.

These islands were M's, truly. The Master kept mostly to himself in the lighthouse, and I was a squatter. M ran the place. We, the two of us, and even that third entity I sometimes caught the Master whispering to, bowed to her whims. When the waters were calm, M could walk on water. At least once or twice, I caught her sunbathing on some of the smallest of the islands with no boat in sight to explain how she got there.

I would do anything for her, even if there were no Master to command me. There have been few women in my life, save my mother and a few chums in my earliest childhood, back before the great and unending disasters that hit the continent brought me here. So, perhaps that is part of it. Another part of it is that there's little to do now that I no longer have a land to rule, and in truth there wasn't much to do when I ruled only myself, and the puffins—and the puffins in their collective strength and ignorance always ignored my dictates.

That's another joke. I am a man; I am not a beast with the power to speak with other beasts.

And indeed, there is just something about M that impels me.

My hut is pretty nice, though M has endlessly refused to visit me here; but it is a space where I can contemplate her without interruption by some task or chore, without the Master trying to pry into my mind. M is the star of all the pornographies in my mind, the protagonist of all my daydreams.

In one of my favorite daydreams, the moon is super full and close to the Earth—it cuts through the endless fog like a spotlight in the rafters, and paints the walls of my hut blue, just as my illuminated screen does, but somehow everything is more beautiful. M doesn't announce her presence with her usual cry of "Mister Kalivas!" or walk in through the door, or even rattle the knob. She scratches at the window with her sea-green painted nails, and her nervous expression melts into a smile when I look up and meet her gaze.

When the scratching at the window actually occurred, it sounded nothing as I imagined it would. The lightest of touches, then a thump. Nor did I respond as I always imagined I would, rising from the bed, the muscles of my chest complimented and my little pooch of a belly hidden by the chiaroscuro lighting in my hut. I yelped and covered myself, then nearly fell from my bed.

It wasn't her. It wasn't the Master. Even had it been someone I'd met before, and I've met almost nobody, I wouldn't have been able to say whom it was scratching at my window, because most of his face had been chewed off by birds.

3

My hut was too nice for this business of flesh and blood. I took the man in the hoop house instead, so he wouldn't create such a mess beyond the capacity of my vacuum and scent-sprayer, and because he had begun to thrash when I led him toward the smokehouse. His tongue was gone, but his croaked objections and bony-fingered smacks were sufficiently communicative.

As if I would strip the flesh from the bones of a man in his state! All the best meats—the cheeks, the rump, the calves, were already gone. But he was not in his right mind, the poor fellow.

In the hoop house he wiggled free of me and dove toward one of the containers in which I had some potatoes growing. They were young and small, but he dug for them and mashed them into his mouth and against what was left of his skin. He wasn't human, not according to my definition, though of course he wore clothes and likely had facility and experience with using and perhaps even making tools. Now he just used his hands and teeth and the artificial inedible tube that was his throat, though.

"¿Te gustaría que te enterrara en la compostera?" I asked him to no response. I offered again, in English, to bury him in the compost, but he just pointed to the gash on the side of his head where his right ear used to be, and shrugged. Then he smiled a very potato-y smile. Little bits rolled off his chin and down his collar and vest.

He was a mainlander, one of those who, like the Master and little M, could not die. Not easily anyway. It would take some time for him to regenerate his nose, his left eye, his ears, the sweetmeats of his face. He had made it to shore in time; the birds hadn't gotten past his dermis, which was probably stronger in the first place than what their beaks had evolved to rend. He was lucky that the ashy storm-petrels were nocturnal, and the cormorants relatively few. He would not have found me without his eyes, wouldn't have been able to smile so goofily with his face gone, and the exposed muscle and bone would have grown so infected so quickly that he'd never have recovered—it would have taken him hours to expire, at the bottom of the Bay, had he managed to inhale as he sank under the waves.

As he stood, I had to watch him shove my precious crops—he was on to the zucchini now, and eyeing the yams with his one good one—into his mouth and rub mashed vegetable matter against his limbs, his belly. He was already heating up, the sweat was steaming off him, the plastic sheeting of my small hoop house fogging over.

The Master would notice that. For a moment I thought of grabbing my shovel, smacking him over the head, and burying him in the compost anyway. He'd either heal faster and could throw himself on the Master's mercy without me, or just expire in the pile.

"You were in the wreck," I said instead. I admit to not being much of a conversationalist. Lack of practice.

He wrote with his finger on the dirt floor the word *storm*, then *sudden*.

Then he wrote *the others*.

They could be anywhere. You washed up, or climbed up onto, the best island. We have buildings, even some from the twentieth century.

His eye went wide at that. I thought he was impressed with the physical plant, but he scratched at the dirt with his finger again, and I saw that his nail was steel, which explained why his scratching at my window sounded so unlike my wildest dream, and then he had a question for me:

WE?

4

How did I become a slave to the Master? He has technology embedded in his body, his palms, that makes him extremely dangerous. At first, though, he enticed me with his babe in arms, M. I'd not seen a child that young since I was nearly that young, and was starved for company of any sort for much of my life. The tragedy of meeting the Master is that even without coercion and torture, I likely would have done almost anything for him, or at least with him.

We cared for the babe together. He was and is a vital man despite his age, with the posture of a redwood tree. The little family amazed me. They could drink the seawater without ill-effect, and the Master even joked that the salt of it "recharged his batteries." They had come to my islands via glider, but an uncrewed submersible had followed them, and the Master dwelled within it for the first several months with the child. I lingered nearby, hoping for conversation, and once even offered the use of my hut, though at the time it was dilapidated.

"You can do something else for me," the Master told me. It was cold, thanks to the season and the wind, but he never shivered, never blinked against the stinging of the salty air. "Bring me a suckling seal pup, fresh off the teat."

I didn't want to. There were plenty of seal pups, and I had no qualms about occasionally hunting a weak adolescent—the adult males were too fierce, the females simply too large for me to eat without wasting most of the meat—but I still didn't want to take an infant from her mother.

"I need the milk," the Master explained. "For little M. I doubt we'd be able to gain the cooperation of an elephant seal to express into a bucket, and elephant seal milk is fatty, like a pudding. So, I need a well-fed pup to slice open, to remove the milk from its gastrointestinal system before it absorbs the nutrients. Fresh off the teat, Kalivas, do you understand?" He spoke the last words in Greek: Kalivas, *katalavaínete*, like it was a little song, and he of course addressed me informally.

Elephant seal mothers don't move much while nursing; nor do they eat or drink. The bulls are wary, but only a few of them truly care in that animal way males care, about the fate of the pups—these newborns were the result of the previous year's breeding. A few alphas breed most of the cows, and the rest of the bull elephants take to lingering solitude and jealous staring. Perhaps the Master could have done this dirty work himself, but he was old and had a child. The seals were used to my smell. I could approach easily.

I crouched several yards away, relieved that the Master had asked this of me now, at the beginning of the season. Even a week later, the pups would be too large to manhandle easily. I imagined that a single pup would be sufficient for however many months little M would need to nurse and that the Master would dilute the viscous milk.

When a pup, the smallest of three, unlatched, I ran to it, grabbed it by the tail, and yanked it backward along the earth. The mother seal peered at me, unable to move and helpless, two other pups still suckling. I suppose she could have bellowed, or smacked her flippers against the ground, but in truth her black-olive gaze seemed to me to be a bit grateful that I eased her burdens.

I killed the pup with my knife, and wrapped the wound in a bit of cloth in case the blood could somehow come in handy for the Master's plans. Twenty minutes later I stood before him, sweating, arms dead, as rank as a corpse. I put the pup down before him, and sliced it open. He stood ready with a small container. I noticed that I had taken to my knees to do his bidding. He didn't bend down, but instead proffered me the container. I scooped the milk out carefully and handed it to him. The Master's thanks was a grunt.

And yet, after years of solitude, company was welcome, and it was a joy to see M take her first steps a few months later, to pull grass out of her mouth, to tell her the names of the birds and the clouds in three languages. Little M loved me and peppered my face with kisses, despite the wind-scars and pits on my cheeks. The islands weren't mine anymore; they were ours.

That is what I believed. The Master did not trick me; M did not beguile me. I lied to myself, that a man such as I could be equal to these beings from the exalted lands twenty-six miles and a million years away.

"Kalivas!" the Master called to me one day. Now that M could walk and talk, he was planning on dismantling his submersible and moving onto the land and into the lighthouse, which I was to help him prepare for long-term occupancy. He would also fix up my hut. That was the deal, a deal between equals, though between the two of us, only one could make his voice sound anywhere on the island.

I rushed to where I knew him to be, atop the cliff that hung over the tiny cove in which the submersible was docked.

"Where's M?" I asked. His face, which had been plain and unblinking like a lizard's, shifted.

"No 'Hello.' No greeting except to ask after my daughter," he said with a sneer. "Kalivas, do you understand?" No singsong this time. "Do you understand who I am, who my daughter is, and why we are here?"

"Of course I do. You're from the mainland. You fell from favor. You're...advanced."

"Yes," said the Master. "We were exiled here. You, little man in your little hut, somehow escaped the notice of my enemies, escaped my notice as well. We thought these islands were uninhabited. They're meant to be uninhabited."

"What's your point?" We were equals. I could be short with an equal if I wished to be. The Master was advanced, but he still depended on me to feed his child, prepare his home. He was weak at times. Once I even caught him with his eyes closed, teetering on his feet as though he were about to swoon. The advanced ones, the non-humans, generally don't sleep. They never sleep, my mother told me.

"You'll not be repopulating this land."

"I...what?"

"I see how you look at my daughter, how you fawn

over her. And I know how patient you are, how patient you must be to have lived here alone all these years before my arrival." My, not our.

"She is going to grow, mature, faster than you know. You're not to touch her. Not to think of her."

She was a child. Truth be told, I never even imagined M growing up, or me growing old, or anything beyond the next season when perhaps the cold would be less biting and we could swim to the smaller islands, explore them, find bird eggs for the Master. But now that the Master mentioned that one day M, who was maturing much faster than I understood humans to do, would be a woman...

I felt a sudden warmth in my chest. Then fire. I was on my knees again, my back, screaming and tearing at my chlamys, at my own flesh. The Master had his palm out, then clenched his hand into a fist, and then the pain stopped. It was as though my pectoral muscles were filled with soothing ice.

"Men such as you are mostly water. I boiled some of it." He held out his palm again. I'd seen the metal embedded in it before, a circle the size of a small coin. The Master had used it in the past to activate various screens on the submersible by waving his palm over them. He had a number of such devices lining his limbs, but I'd no idea they could serve as weapons. "Microwaves. There will be no unpleasant smells, no burnt clothing, no permanent damage to the epidermis, just pain, and if I decide to focus on your brain, death. Do you understand?"

I said nothing, but I did understand. I spent my life on these rocks. I had strong legs. I was a hunter. But all he had to do was wave a hand at me. He never slept, hardly ever anyway, but I would have to close my eyes eventually, and who knows in what condition I'd wake up. Missing an eye, or my nose—he needed my limbs.

"I asked you a question," the Master said, opening his palm again and gesturing toward my groin. I screamed like a prey animal.

It's been thirteen years.

5

The Master must have known of the wrecked ship already, so there was no need for me to tell him. Not a breeze passes over the islands without him knowing. But these shipwrecked men and women were like him—advanced, with tiny machines of the sort my mother once developed and commanded swimming in their bones. Perhaps they had the means to hide themselves from him, or thought they did, but the rain took them by surprise.

Perhaps I could go back and kill the man, snap his ulnae and radii and slurp down the nano-rich marrow, let the machines colonize me. If only things were so simple.

And speaking of not simple, M was on the water. She climbed the swells like someone scrambling over a hill, her red hair plastered against her back. So that's how she does it. I didn't understand the Master's technology, but I could guess that the coin-sized implants in her palms and arms, along her legs and on the bottom of her feet, allowed her to crawl across the surface of the water somehow, even though the chop was rough and littered with debris.

But then her arms fell through the waves, then her head. She wriggled her way back out of the water, then purposefully pushed her hand under the surface. Something pulled at her, but she righted herself and up came a man. They threw their arms around one another, and M bobbed up above the water again, making the sea into foam as her technology strained against the extra weight of the waterlogged fellow.

M couldn't sink her legs beneath the waves, and couldn't pull the man onto the surface of the water either. Perhaps he lacked the implants she had, despite the fact that he obviously was not-all-human—much of his flesh was gone, or discolored and sloughing off, and I could see silver and copper glinting in spots along his torso and arms. She crawled ahead, toward the far end of the cove, nudging the man with her head.

Inventive, determined, compassionate. M was everything. The perfect person. The child who never cried, the girl who didn't need to pout, as the world belonged to her. And now the woman who had found herself a broken man to fix and possess.

I could not imagine the Master sending M out to perform this rescue. She must know something the Master does not. Does she have access to that unseen entity to whom the Master so often mutters? Could that being be the Master's master, the slavemaster's own owner?

M was a powerful swimmer, but she was not truly swimming, rather just ambulating, and keeping the second body from sinking while she crawled with three limbs along the surface of the water, so while she traveled in a straight line across to the far side of the cove away from the lighthouse, she made poor time. I took off in a crouching run, running along but some yards distant from the shore.

It was a near thing, but I managed to be standing over the thin spit of sandy land on the other side of the cove by the time M emerged from the water with her prize. Strong, she carried him in her arms, though he was twice her size and indeed probably a head taller than me. I tried to stand upright, to look collected, but I had to put my hands on my knees. I smiled through a fit of wheezing, and M smiled back.

"A survivor! Isn't he incredible!" she called out to me, waving the man in her arms at me as though he were a magnificent fish.

"How did you find him? What were you even doing by the shore?"

"Looking at the wreckage swirling around in the cove," M said. She knelt and let the man slide down her arms and onto the sand. He was as ruined as the fellow currently in my hoop house—a corpse that could heal, or repair itself, thanks to the same machines that made the Master so fierce and M so incredible.

"And your father?"

"In the lab. The lab, always in the lab," she said. She looked down at her feet, so adorable and white, her toes like tiny eggs from tiny birds I'd crunch between my teeth, shell and all.

No, it was the ruined half-corpse at her feet that held her interest. "I want to keep him. Will you help me, Mister Kalivas?"

"Your father would not approve."

"Why do you think I'm asking for your help?" she said. It wasn't really a question. She smiled the smile she always gave me as a child, all teeth and squinting. "You need to keep him in the hut. Make him a Kalivas too. A little family. Heh heh, get it?"

M didn't get much chance to talk to anyone save me and the Master, so her sense of humor was a bit stunted. She didn't even have the screen full of dramas and pornographies that I had. For her, the joke that Kalivas, the Greek surname, meant "hut" was the height of comedy, given that I indeed lived in what they had decided to call a hut.

"I get it," I said. "But what's in it for me? You're asking me to take a great risk, Miss." M is for a lot of things. I only ever address her as Miss, when I call her anything at all.

"What's in it for you?" She was utterly confused. "I'm telling you to do it. That's what you do. What I say you should do; what my father says you should do. It's always been thus."

"Your father doesn't want these people here."

"Maybe he does!"

"If you think so," I told M, "why don't I grab this man's legs and you take his arms and we walk him over to yonder lighthouse, where your father is in his lab, as you say. Working together, it would take us just thirty minutes if we don't stop and rest, and I'll shoulder more than my share of his weight, so we need not stop and rest."

"I...he doesn't wish to be disturbed, Mister Kalivas. As you well know," M said. "And, wouldn't he just tell you to nurse this man back to health anyway? It would be your job. Everything is already your job. I'm just helping you because I want this man. Take him to be another Mister Kalivas, Mister Kalivas. It's good to show initiative, my father says."

Though he was in a more dire condition than the man in my hoop house, I knew this fellow would eventually reknit himself too, so long as he had access to sunlight and proteins. M would get what M wants.

"But why do you want a man? What would you do with him?" There had previously been an edge in my voice; now there was a crack.

"Unspeakable things!" She guffawed so hard I could practically see her tonsils. "I read that phrase recently in a book. Father's library really is something." She tapped her eye. There was a hard lens covering it; I could hear her fingernail clicking against it. I was tempted for a horrible moment to take a thumb to my own eye, to show her what a real man was, how we were born to suffer, how easy it was to hurt us. "I need some company is all. Once this man is healthy again, I'll learn his name, his life story, tell it to Father."

"Your father is kind and compassionate. He'd let you have a pet." I looked down at the man. He was conscious now, or at least his eyes—as perfect as M's, though bird-wing brown, not drift glass blue—were open and glinted with awareness.

"Perhaps..." M looked down at him too, smiled with only the left half of her mouth. "There are many islands in walking distance. We can secret him on one. I went all the way to the Island of Saint James, once. You know what I saw there?"

"Piles of bird shit?"

"No, well, yes. But also an A-frame. Battered, with holes punched through the roof, but it was a home of some sort. Can you imagine that a person actually lived here once, on Los Farallones?"

"Yes, I can imagine that," I said plainly. M's naïveté was usually endearing.

"I mean, of course, in the olden days many people lived here! Sir Francis Drake, and Helen Mabbott and the

Youess Kostagard and Jimmy Carter, but I mean relatively recently. Within the last fifty years a human being actually settled on the island. I bet they built the shelter out of the hull of their boat."

"If my father doesn't like this man and doesn't want him on our island, I'll just walk him over and show him the A-frame, and he can live here." She clasped her hands together and squeezed them till her shoulders met her precious little earlobes. "It's a splendid idea, Mister Kalivas! You must help me!"

M is for a lot of things. Must, said in the manner of the Master, is one of them.

"I'll call him Francis if when he is healed he doesn't remember his name," M said. "No, I'll call him Francis regardless! Doesn't he look like a Francis to you?"

"I'd need to see more flesh on him in order to say definitively, Miss," I said. Francis smiled up at me, but that might have just been because his lips and chin and most of his cheeks were gone. Naked skulls are always smiling to my eye.

"Fuh fuh fuh," he said. Wonderful. His larynx was regenerating. I'd have *parea*—true company or companionship. Conversations for three, if the man back at the hoop house would continue to grace me with his remarkable penmanship. How utterly wonderful. "Ferr-deh..."

Ferdy?

6

"You have one too!" M cried out when she saw the ruined man resting in my hoop house. In truth, he didn't look as bad as he did just a few hours ago, when I'd left him. Some of the smaller wounds had healed over already, and his eyes had a bit more life in them. The beginnings of a significant message was scraped into the dirt. I immediately walked all over it, manhandling M's new pet-man next to the survivor I found as my excuse for the clumsy stomping around.

"I think mine is better, Mister Kalivas," said M. "Why didn't you tell me you found another person from the shipwreck?"

"I wasn't sure whether you'd approve, or that your father would. In fact, I am sure the Master would not approve at all."

"Yes yes, you said that already. But how could you think such a thing about Daddy? He's only ever been kind to you. "

The washed-away men saved me from having to deal

with M's claim by moaning and crawling toward one another. They clasped hands like long-lost friends, or the lovers in the first, or last, moments of a pornography. M's, Francis or Fuh Fuh Fuh, tried to croak out a few words, but the fellow I found pointed to his own neck and, with a pat of his palm against the air, counseled patience. He turned to look expectantly at me.

"I think our friends want a moment alone," I said to M.

"Of course, of course," M said. She took my hand—she took my hand!—and led me out of my own hoop house.

She turned at the corner and walked halfway down the length of the hoop house and planted herself in a spot not far from where, inside, the two men kneeled and clung to one another. I could see them fairly clearly through the several layers of translucent, if well-battered, plastic sheeting stretched over the skeleton of the hoop house, and M could undoubtedly see and hear them, as if there were no barrier at all.

"We'll spy," said M. "If they turn their heads, they'll see us, of course, but truly, what are they going to do? Shrink away? Reject our hospitality and run back into the ocean?"

"Not say anything compromising?" I suggested. Though what compromising thing they might have to share with one another and not with us I had no idea.

"Is this what a zoological garden was like, or is this more like a snow globe?"

"A bit of both," I told her. "Don't try to shake my hoop house though."

"You're so funny, Mister Kalivas," she said, but she didn't smile or laugh. I lived to make M smile or laugh.

My man scribbled something into the dirt, and M's find nodded as vigorously as he could in response, then pointed at some of the wording, and erased one thing with his palm. The angle was such that we couldn't see what was being argued, but M, made a genius by her father, was able to extrapolate what was being communicated just by carefully watching the movements of their fingers.

"They're talking about me!" she said, so excited that she reached out and pinched my elbow, shaking my arm with her grip. "They know Father; they know who I am. They played with me when I was a baby; they were just kids then themselves, but their fathers knew my father. Oh, that's exciting! It's a small world after all, eh?"

I had known M as a baby too, and much better than these broken machine-men ever could have. She wasn't excited to think of the times I carried her, cooed at her when the wind would make her cry, or when her father would scowl so severely it would cause her physical pain like a shock in her implants. And it was a small world—too small. My mother told me once that even before myriad disasters, the Bay Area always seemed cozier than it should have. We had millions living in our cities when you added them all up, but it was so easy to just bump into a friend or acquaintance. It was as though there were only ninety people living in San Francisco, and they just repeated themselves over and over. That had been one of the many things she had told me about times past, or at least vocalized through the air in my presence.

The punchline was that by the time she evacuated us to the Farallons, there practically were all of ninety people living in the Bay Area. The number wasn't quite accurate, nor was the term people.

I am a person. I am a man. I may be the only one, the only true man, within one thousand miles.

And I was surrounded by beings who were very much not human. There had been two, and now there were four.

7

My mother, Soteria, was a genius. Scientist, CEO, social engineer. She had twin PhDs, one in cell biology, and the other in physics, and she earned them simultaneously, rather than in series. Her true genius was not her scientific acumen, but her business smarts. Soteria had taken advantage of a peculiarity in California by "reading" the law and apprenticing to an attorney in order to become a lawyer herself. Three schools at once would have been too onerous and time-consuming, even for my mother. Her inventions, various forms of bioactive nanotechnology, she developed while in school, but managed to keep for herself as her own intellectual property.

Soteria could have become one of the many billionaires local to the Bay Area, but here is an interesting fact: in the days before the cataclysms, many people were suspicious of women. Even other women were! She kept her inventions mostly to herself and one of her academic advisors, licensing only inferior versions of her trade secrets: telomerase treatments to inhibit cancer, but not biological aging. Embeddable wearable technologies, but not self-replicating open-ended nanotech cultivated in the spinal fluid and distributed through the very marrow of one's bones.

Soteria the Sorceress, the media called her. How humiliating that most public figures were known by their surnames. Mother was humiliated by the casual use of her first name—its pronunciation often mangled by Anglos who refused to roll their r's—in the news and among the gossips and magpies of the Internet.

She also very much disliked being called a sorceress. She'd published well, made posters and presentations for conferences, and filed patents appropriately. What she had made was all there for anyone to see, if only they'd eyes and a mind to. There was no such thing as magic, nor even such thing as a "natural" when it came to math and science. She pointed to herself—the daughter of a pair of immigrants who worked at a university as janitors and thus secured free tuition for their daughter and two mediocre sons—as proof.

It was an eccentric opinion in those days of "tech" professionals somehow becoming celebrities, opinion leaders, and even the rulers of states small and large. If anyone could develop a seemingly preternatural intellect with practice and dedication, then there would be no special cachet to it for the elite; they weren't God's Own Special Boys after all. On the other side of the coin, if anyone could be as smart as Mother, then the endless masses who clearly were not, had done something wrong.

A genius such as my mother could stand up against her fellow geniuses and swat them down, or defend herself against hoi polloi, but not both, not both at once. The world rose up against her, and she chose exile.

This is what she told me as a child, the underlying

themes of the anecdotes about life on the mainstream she shared with me in those few years she raised me here before succumbing to a wasting disease that made her lungs harden and pink filth bubble up between her teeth. She chose exile.

All I remember is being strapped to her back as she swam twenty-six rough miles. I tried to hold in my piss so as not to disturb her stroke, but was too weakened by the calming medicine she gave me to do much more than sleep when I could and spit out salt water after she'd crash into a wave. Soteria Kaliva was incredible—she not only carried me but also pulled behind us a train of rowboats full of supplies tied to her waist with a rope. Her elite enemies would have found us had she used any sort of powered vehicle, and any random fool on a pier would have spotted a sloop or a ketch leaving a port.

It perhaps goes without saying that my mother had taken to assigning herself as a test subject, and her graduate advisor as a control, when engaging in some of her experiments on improving the human body via nanotechnological and biochemical means.

But I, her son, am human. My hut, a folding thing, came from her boats, as did my database of entertainments, heirloom seeds, the solar cells, the desalinator that provides potable water, and much of the rest. She taught me many things in the few years we had together, but I could only ever understand the rudiments of the science that had made her the Sorceress of Silicon Valley. I was but a child, two years younger than M is now, though I grew up far more slowly, with barely the strength to follow my mother's instructions to bury her in the compost and await her resurrection, which never came.

I do not know my father.

8

The Master had made himself scarce for several days. I was lonely enough for sensible company that I got it into my head to go look for him. The island on which we live is small enough that it is more or less impossible to hide, and the submersible had long since been reduced to a few plates left to rust, so he must have secreted himself on one of the smaller islands in our chain. The Master could walk on water, and was better at it than M. Perhaps he had manufactured a tent, or was staying in the A-frame.

I was also half-tempted to let M take her Francis to the A-frame, just to see what would happen. I remember seeing a fireworks show as a child one Fourth of July at the Berkeley Marina. It was astounding, a war against the very dome of night, and I cried, and for hours everything smelled like Hell. The Master would put on such a show for me if he encountered his daughter and a strange male, especially while on retreat.

I couldn't walk the swells between the islands, but I knew someone who possibly could.

Speaking of strange males.

"Stefano." I announced myself upon entering my hut, and Stefano, who had made himself a nest of my bed's blankets, was running four different pornographies at once on my screens and also eating one of my potatoes, raw, looked up.

"Monstruo!" he cried, his cheeks puffy with my food. He was regenerating quickly, though he was still weak, still afraid of me. I was happy to answer to Monster. M is for a lot of things.

"I've interrupted your convalescence." I squatted on the floor, my legs crossbones-style under me, my hands on my knees. I'd found that this posture calmed Stefano. "It's time for you to start earning your keep." I collected a few odds and ends—forks, a wayward sock belonging to Stefano, a paperback book he'd been looking at, two pencils, and a few other items—and arranged them as best I could as a map of the Farallon Islands.

"I am but your proximate host. The ultimate host, the father of my dearest friend, has not been seen since you were plucked out of the sea," I told him. Stefano did not look calm at all, but he stayed silent despite his agitation. "I believe he has traveled to one of the other islands. Only a few are anything other than rocks jutting out of the water, but he may be on one of these..."

"Do you know..." Stefano asked me, "anything?"

"You're living in my home. I know that much," I said.

"Do you even know who that man is? What he's capable of?"

"I am familiar." I decided that I'd liked Stefano better back when the birds had taken his throat.

"Then why do you want to find him? Isn't my company sufficient?"

I shrugged the shrug I'd seen comical children perform on my screen. Stefano didn't get it.

"If he's gone from this island, what we should be doing is working together to keep him off of it. If he's on another island, we should destroy it, let him be buried fifty fathoms deep, under a thousand tons of rock."

"You don't like him very much. What has he ever done to you?"

"He was our leader, once. The very King of the Bay. We neutralized his tech, sent him and his baby out on a glider in the hope that he'd just plummet into the sea. We had no idea he'd land here, much less thrive."

Perhaps they didn't know about the submersible. The Master may have arranged for it to pace him, almost the same way my own mother, decades earlier, had towed supplies and equipment behind her as she swam to these islands.

"A glider can't be hacked," Stefano explained to me unnecessarily.

"It can be piloted. A man with a babe in arms has significant motivation to find a way to live."

"He was supposed to *live*"—Stefano even made a gesture to suggest the operative word in quotation marks —"in the drink, to be torn apart by sharks, kept apart by the currents."

"The baby too?" I had the thought to take Stefano across my shoulders as he slept and put him back in the water to keep the cormorants fed.

"His choice. She was a baby; she could still die. We weren't going to raise her as anything other than a person of flesh and blood. He'd rather she died." It was his turn to shrug, and his was a regal display of resignation. "That didn't happen either. I'm happy to say, you see! She's a delightful girl!"

"Delightful-looking you mean," I said. "You have not spoken to her." In a way, I was asking Stefano a question.

"I'm sure she's as beautiful inside as she is out." He was asking me a question now. One I saw no reason to answer. "Ach, anyway, have two men have nothing better to discuss than a woman?"

"I came to discuss..." I dared not call the Master the Master before Stefano. "Him."

"He was a tyrant. He ruled over us with an iron thumb, or whatever the old-timey figurative phrase is. We were well rid of him. The community in San Francisco has blossomed since his exec-...ex...exile. I guess it was never truly an execution, and indeed he is in exile now. And has, according to you, exiled himself even further, to a smaller and more tedious locale!"

He lowered himself back onto my bed and rested his head on my pillow and peered up at the dome of my ceiling. "And now you wish to find him again."

"You can swim. You won't die," I said.

"You can't even swim? Animals can swim, Kalivas!"

I ignored the bundle of connotations that utterance was wrapped in. "I can swim in calmer waters. Since the great storm that brought you here, the waves have been high. I could swim to Maintop Island, and perhaps in calmer seas, swim out to the little pimple, take my rest, and then swim on to the islands of the north, but I don't know if I'd be able to make it back safely."

"If you interrupt whatever he is doing, you certainly won't make it back safely." Stefano raised himself on one elbow, placed his cheek atop his fist, and peered at me in a way nobody had ever peered at me before. In truth, this conversation was the first I'd ever had with anyone within a decade of my own age—Stefano was a peer to me, even as he was a'peerin' at me. "You're in good shape for a free-range human. How old are you?" he asked me, then answered his own question. "Some wear and tear, but you're outdoorsy. There's hardly any indoors here. You said you knew M as a baby? What are you, forty?"

"Thirty-six."

"I'm thirty," Stefano said. "I regret every second over twenty-five. You know, we can decide our own ages, those who get the implants early enough. That's what drove the Prosperous One so mad. He was already old when he mastered the technology. He couldn't age backward..." He screwed up his lips and snorted. "Well, except for his sperm!"

"The Prosperous One."

"It was a joke—he was rich when there was money, and tried to keep it going. Money, that is! As if we would all start trading it again to humor him! A community of a few thousand, we eat largely for entertainment purposes and have an entire city built up for 700,000 people to dwell in. We don't really need such a thing. It's the same here, I'm sure. Do you have any money?"

"No, but I have food, and you've eaten more than your share," I said.

"As I said, largely for entertainment purposes, but food is useful raw material for regeneration as well."

"My understanding," I said, "is that San Francisco and the surrounding cities were destroyed in earthquakes. Fires. Mudslides. Tens of thousands of people died. Then came the great viruses again, and the water turned brackish—"

He held up a palm, rolled his eyes, like a character in a show. "Ugh. Yes. Stop. History is the worst. The point is this: let's say that one building in fifty was habitable, and there was enough embedtech to keep a relative handful of survivors hale and hearty indefinitely, and I do mean indefinitely. Okay, homes and offices for seventy thousand, all free for use. And only perhaps two thousand people in all the land—everyone fucking, but nobody birthing, except for Thee Prosperous One."

"This is all a lot to tell me just to keep from doing me the tiny favor of helping me locate him," I said.

"Babies and cash! He's so old-fashioned! Like something out of a melodrama!" Stefano cried, hand to his heart.

"I'm going to set my bed on fire if you don't get up and help me. I'll keep your ankles and wrists tied to pegs in my garden, and eat your internal organs. I'll have a regular meat harvest every two months. I won't have to hunt the lion seal or try to domesticate the seagull." I peered at him in the way he had peered at me moments earlier, like a naked man in a pornography looking at another just before the tongues came out.

"You couldn't," Stefano said.

"You're still weak," I said. "I could."

"Perhaps I'm so weak I couldn't manage the swim."

"Try," I said. "Do it for me. Or you'll do something else for me. You'll provide casings for my sausage, for the rest of my life."

"You wouldn't. It's not..."

"Civilized?"

I smiled with my teeth, to show him that I was hungry.

"What island is he most likely to be on?" Stefano said, sighing.

I pointed to the pencil furthest from the paperback book.

9

The sky had turned purple, then slate gray, before Stefano crawled back over the waves to report his failure. I was thinking like the Master now—it was hardly Stefano's fault that I had guessed wrong, but still, the failure was his, not mine.

Obviously the failure was his. His skin was white as bone, his hair a mess, his eyes red with salt, and he even trailed some seaweed tied around one ankle. If I were him, I would have slayed me where I stood, which was at the lip of the cove. I would have snatched me up by my ankles and dragged myself into the sea, planted myself deep in the sand and let the sharks have me.

I was the one who could die, after all. The one who would die, and quickly.

"Bracing!" Stefano said. He was peculiarly happy. Perhaps he realized that if he could make the swim around the inlets, he had the strength to murder me. "Fucking December, Kalivas!"

"I got cold waiting for you," I said. "Since you've

returned, I presume you've not encountered the, uh, Prosperous One."

"Lucky us." He smiled and gestured for my blanket. I took it off my shoulders and wrapped it around his. "Do you know what this means? The island is ours now! Let's get to the lighthouse!"

"The cold has frozen your brain," I said.

"It's not. The Prosperous One isn't there, is he?"

"He indeed is not."

"And he wasn't there among the Devil's Teeth!" Stefano said, waving toward the barely visible silhouettes of the inlets and islands in the distance. "So he's gone! Perhaps into the briny deep, perhaps he built a wondrous flying machine when you weren't looking and is making a run for the Republic of Los Angeles, where I hear they still trade in gold pressed into the shapes of stars the size of your head. Or maybe he's just napping on one of the northern islands you didn't ask me to check—and thank you for your *thank you*, which I am still waiting for—but regardless, he is not here. And we are. You know what I mean?"

"What do you mean, Stefano?"

"Where there's a slot, be a tab, I always say. Let's take the lighthouse, Kalivas."

My experience with the enhanced thus far was limited to the Master, and M. M was a young person, though a precocious genius, and the Master's intellect was unfathomable. He was near a match to my mother, though of course her brain was almost entirely organic until those final days when we made our escape. But Stefano...

"Have you always been like this, Stefano?" I asked as I followed him. He had tied my blanket around his neck clumsily, to make a cape, and was marching directly onward to the lighthouse.

"Audacious? Decisive? A man of ambition and destiny?"

"Certainly the first two and perhaps a dash of the third..." His body was incredible. Already the color and vigor had returned to his limbs, and he strode, his feet bare and caked in mud, up the damp incline with a confidence I could never muster. I was a crouching, flinching thing in the best of times, which is why the Master and M both despised me.

And yet: "Perhaps you don't think things through as you should?" Hours before, I had terrorized this man, and now he was bold and forthright like a marble statue of an ancient god—you know, rock-headed. "Is that an artifact of your regenerative abilities? You're nigh invulnerable, it seems. Perhaps, perhaps, I couldn't have eaten you as I threatened this afternoon. It's just that when you use my bed, I must sleep on the floor, and I've grown used to the Master..."

I gasped at myself. Not only was I babbling, but I'd let slip my name for the man Stefano contemptuously called The Prosperous One.

"The Master!" Stefano obviously liked the way those words felt in his mouth, on his tongue.

"I've grown used to his face."

"I'll bet!" Stefano crowed. "So, if you're a slave, then you should be thrilled with my glorious idea. Liberation! Let's take over, the two of us!"

"You'd spend your endless life here, ruling over the gulls and the sea lions, even after I grow old and die?"

Stefano stopped in his tracks, then turned to me with a flourish of his cape. "If there is one thing I've learned as a member of the court—when you see an open spot in a position higher than your own, snag it! Also, I'm sure between the two of us...and the Master's surely wondrous cache of technology, we can build an autogyro before you shuffle off this mortal coil." He started walking again, toward the lighthouse, knowing that I would follow without needing to signal to me that I should.

"Hmm," I said. "Is that how you all think, over on the mainland?"

He kept walking, and laughed. "Now that you mention it, no! I tell you, my brush with incapacitation has changed me. Most of my life, I was sober, straight, perhaps even humble, you might say. It must be the island breezes, or those cold hours being pecked to shreds in the salted sea, that have me fired up!"

"What do you think the girl and Fuh-Fuh-Francis have gotten up to?"

That query stilled his incredible legs.

"Is she your woman?" he asked. There was some music in his voice. Stefano practically sang every utterance now that he could speak again, and had something delicious to gossip about.

"She is not." The words spilled from my mouth painfully. I wanted to sound offended, and nonchalant, and definitive all at once, but ended up sounding to my own ears just strangled and plaintive. "Absolutely not."

His tongue a knife, Stefano said, plainly for once, "I can see why." He gestured toward the lighthouse, making his cape flap. "Onward!"

I'd not spent much time in the lighthouse since M entered puberty. It occurred to me now that I did not know exactly how old she was—with the Master's technology embedded in her, she, or more likely he, could retard or accelerate her development, both physical and mental. These men, with their chronometers and memories of M's birth and exile, would know, should know...

The door to the brief two-story radio building, where

M usually kept herself, was unlocked. Why would anyone lock it?

"Well!" Francis exclaimed. "What's this then?" He was seated on the ancient couch in the poorly appointed front room next to M. On their laps—their knees were touching—they shared one of the Master's several ancient texts. Collector's items or the like. These beings had all the information they could possibly ever need already inscribed into their brains. "Stefano!"

"Ferdy!"

"It's Francis," said M. "Oh, hullo Mister Kalivas."

They all turned to me. This was the first time in memory I had ever been in the presence of three sentient beings. Something shimmered in the air of the small, dank room. Couldn't they smell the mold? Wasn't the wood of the floor annoyingly soft under their feet?

"What are you doing?" I asked, too harshly.

"What are *you* doing?" asked M.

"Oh," I said. I pointed to Stefano. "He's here to take over. Stefano here will depose your father, claim all of your family possessions as his own, and rule over this island. Benevolently."

"Benevolently," Francis said. His name was certainly not Francis, but M had her opinions, and I chose to follow her lead.

"Naturally, benevolently," said Stefano.

M slid her father's book from Francis's lap onto hers, then shut it. "You'll do no such thing, sir," she said to Stefano. Then she looked at me. "Seize him."

We all looked at her—the men—and then we looked at one another. Francis smiled widely—he had a big face that held a huge mouth, more like a potato split down the middle than any animal I'd ever beheld. Stefano, so confident as he led me to his new stronghold, pulled my blanket around himself to hide his body.

"Kalivas!" cried M. "Get with the seizing!" Without thinking, I reached out with my right arm and took hold of Stefano's elbow. He moved against me, so I grabbed his wrist as well and stepped behind him. With a twist, I locked his wrist, his elbow, his shoulder, and much of his spine. He bowed, grunted, but did not squeal.

"How dare you try to take over mi Farallones!" M said. She flew from the couch, calling that she'd be right back, and ran through the door that led to the lighthouse proper.

"Kalivas, I could fling you through the wall if I so desired," said Stefano, "but then my kingdom would lack a subject. Let me go before she comes back."

"She's not going far," I said.

"And I'm very fast," M said, back already from replacing her father's precious book. "And don't you let him go, Mister Kalivas. Francis, explain your friend to me! He's a rabble-rouser, a revolutionary! How could you hang out with the likes of him?"

Francis laughed again. "He's not a revolutionary. He's the first son of the duke I was telling you of. The Duke of San Francisco, whose yacht we were on when the storm hit."

"The sons of the elite often make the best revolutionaries," I said.

"No, the sons of the elite make the most common revolutionaries," M said. "The key word being common. Pull his head up by his hair, Mister Kalivas, I want to spit right in his face."

"I don't think that's necessary," Stefano said. I said it too, right after.

"Francis, how do you deal with revolutionaries in the

city for which you are named?" M demanded to know. She had her fists on her hips now, and was glaring at us all. She had never been in a room with three males before. Truly, this was an evening of firsts.

"We don't have revolutionaries. My name isn't Francis. I keep telling you that, Mandy," Francis said. "But we don't have revolutionaries. The AI—the AI...Stefano?"

Stefano grinned. I tightened my hold to melt that smile into a grimace, and for a moment it worked, but he relaxed his shoulder, smiled again, and found an angle to push back against my grip. I'd been defeated, and he had hardly moved. He could fling me to the ground whenever he wished, but chose to stay stooped over, his arm angled against his back.

"'Bout time you noticed," Stefano said. "We're free."

"We are free," Francis said. He stretched regally in his seat on the couch, crossed his legs at the ankles, and laced his fingers behind his head. "This is what I was trying to explain, Mandy."

"Our friends are broken, Mister Kalivas," M said. "They hear voices."

"Heard voices," Stefano said. And with a wriggle he was free, and behind me, with my wrist in his right hand and his left palm against my elbow, and he could have not just locked my joints, but removed my arm entirely, like pulling the wings from a bird after its hour on the spit.

"It's all very romantic when you put it that way, Stefano, all absinthe and madhouses. A small society of people who do not really need one another to sustain life would tend to drift apart, so Stefano's father had the wonderful idea of networking all of us to increase our empathy, our sympathy, and to enhance the superego of each person."

"My father has put the super in superego, you see," said Stefano.

"We'd be orangutans without Stefano's father," Francis said. "Virtually asocial as a species. Meeting only occasionally. To fuck." He made sure to train his gaze on M for those last two words. I would have sacrificed my arm to have his throat, but Stefano had grapevined one of his legs about mine while his friend spoke, so I couldn't even rush across the room.

"The voice they hear is a computer. It tells them things—how to behave, how to survive. It's a bit like a conscience, I suppose. But it's artificial, and it has a mind of its own," said M. "Such creatures!"

"So you can see, we've nobody to tell us what to do now," said Francis.

"Ah, that explains the brainwave ol' Stefano here had a couple of hours ago when he leapt out of my bed. He—"

"Your bed," Francis interrupted.

"—wishes to conquer these islands, and displace your father, Miss M," I finished. "And I'm to be his lieutenant. Isn't that so, Stefano?"

"Is that so, Stefano," she said. It wasn't a question. I could smell the sudden burst of perspiration coming from her form; it hit me like a wave. All of her blushed.

"I don't recall appointing any lieutenants, but I think we can all agree that Kalivas here—" he cranked up the twisting pressure on my arm, but I did not grunt as he wanted me to—"would be excellent. He knows the islands very well; he is very appreciative of you, young Miss, and would do nothing to harm you, I am sure...well, reasonably sure, and he saved me from months of misery and torture. For that, I will always hold him in the highest esteem." Stefano let me go and stepped back, his palms raised. "We should be your lieutenants, Kalivas!" Stefano exclaimed. Francis guffawed at that, and M stared at me.

I wasn't going to turn the offer down, dubious as it was. These islands were mine. The bones of my mother are buried here, and one day, it will be she who will return, as she has promised. And the simple fact is that if this pair of posthuman men wanted the islands, and even M, for themselves, they would have it all, and I'd have little power to stop them. But if the voices in their heads have abandoned them, then perhaps they cannot tell a well-considered idea from a fanciful notion, and they might indeed make king, el rey, o vasilias—however anyone might say it.

"I humbly accept," I said. "And indeed, Stefano here will be my chief lieutenant, and Francis my second lieutenant."

"And I'll be your queen," M said, and she ran to me and flung her arms about me and smelled so sweet, like the orange poppies I remembered from childhood, and the soap I once owned years ago, and spiced cake, which I had just one Christmas before the world ended, and she kissed the lobe of my ear for a just a moment like an insect landing on a bubble on the water and then alighting as it pops and by all rights, after all I faced in my life, after the death of my mother and more than a decade of solitude and years of torture at the hands of the Master and all else I'd faced it should have lasted forever and forever, it should have been real and meant anything at all.

10

Island life with Mother, her sorceress technology notwithstanding, was hard. We were alone save for the wildest of animals and a roiling sea. In the first weeks, we lived in a tent and ate old rations, except when my mother liberated some eggs and scrambled them. She built the hut in which I still live, and my smokehouse from material she brought with us and with appropriated materials from the few shacks on the island.

"There's just enough here," she said, more to herself than me. "Just enough." Mother had surveilled the Southeast Farallon Island with a drone beforehand—it was a set of cookware abandoned in the twentieth century that cemented her decision to escape Saint Francis and come to this place. The drone, its solar cells, and its four motors were cannibalized like everything else to create the suite of technology I have at my disposal to this day.

We soon transitioned to eating the seal, the shark, and the gull. I missed hamburgers and sodas, but my mother did grow some potatoes, so we had French fries on occasion. It hardly mattered what Mother ate; virtually any organic substance would suffice, thanks to the many adjustments she'd made to herself. I, on the other hand, had to keep to an appropriate diet for a growing boy. I needed to stay inside when it rained and by the fire when it was cold, and I had to sleep at night. My mother was awake twenty-four hours a day, and could withstand the elements even fully nude, which she often was. Packing clothes would have wasted space, and repairing them, time.

She did keep two outfits though, for the day we were to return to the mainland, after the political situation that led to her exile blew over. That was always the plan, that is what Mother always told me. We would return one day; Soteria in victory, and her baby boy a fine young man, muscled like a savage but with the mind of a savant. The Greek Ideal.

Once the hut was completed and a daily routine of education, gathering, and fishing was cemented, my mother spent much of her time with her screens, in the radio room adjacent to the lighthouse. Mostly the island was quiet save for the birds and the waves, which I admit is like saying war is mostly silent save for the screaming and the explosions—but it's true. War is mostly silent, and so was the island, but there were times when I'd hear my mother in the radio room, reading aloud, chanting numbers, sharing lengthy anecdotes with nobody. I knew she wasn't transmitting; she explained to me that she was only recording. For me. For when I was older, to help me understand the world.

When she grew ill, I asked about the recordings, but she didn't answer. She didn't smile a maternal smile, nor did she have any comforting words, or a peculiar yet gnomic utterance for me to puzzle over. She yelled at me to pound on her back, to break into her tiny store of pills we had kept otherwise untouched for years, and to shut the fuck up and carry her back to the hut.

That was the last six months of her life. My loving if occasionally oblivious mother, who had cooed over me and pet my hair when I was sick—she was never sick!—who had taught me to perform mental math and how to hunt, who had left me alone to view pornographies when I entered the developmental stage where I'd be curious. Now she'd drag herself to the radio room, and come back to the hut to wheeze out her demands. She called me names, slapped me across the face when I spilled something or moved too slowly, and told me never to raise my hands, never even flinch.

"Stand there and take it!" Mother's teeth were always clenched. "Don't you dare fight back or try to escape!"

Despite her weakness, her hand was still strong and wide, just as it was when she swam nearly thirty miles with me on her back and a train of rowboats in tow. Though I was a teen, a new man, and my mother a woman in swift decline, I was no match for her. And she had raised me, been the only human being in my life. There was nothing for me to do. Despite her illness, she still never slept, but now the nights were filled with the air-tearing noise of her dry cough rather than the susurrations of small chores and subtle intellectual labor. And she howled at me, with those crippled lungs—orders, insults, and cries for the world that had thrown her away.

Most often I led her to the radio room at dawn and sat on the grass outside till the sky went pink and purple. Mother would emerge and I'd carry her on my back to the hut and put her down to rest. The bed was all hers in those final months. I slept on the floor. You might expect me to say curled up, but no, I always flung my limbs wide like a sea star. Mother was too weak to even get up in the night and step on me. She relieved herself in one of the original cookpans that had made these islands so attractive to her.

The last week was the best, as I finally understood that she was truly going to die, her ingenious inventions notwithstanding. I didn't know what had failed, and it was clear that she did not know either. She insisted that she was going to succeed in her grand project, that she would retake the mainland and I would be her heir.

The last morning was the very best, as for once the clouds broke and the sea seemed calmer. Like many people do just before they pass, my mother seemed to rally. She cooked us eggs that morning, fried seal bacon to go with it, and used some of her precious store of peppercorns for seasoning. We exchanged pleasant conversation about the weather, and she even had the computer play some music. It was nothing I was familiar with. Normally, Mother found melodies distracting—it pulled her out of her purely mathematical mindset and the problems she was working on—and there was no one else to curate selections or train me in what was good and what was bad. I did not develop a taste for music until long after my mother's death.

Birds have songs too, but the birds here, great swarms of them, are uniformly unpleasant.

When the sun was high, she walked outside to the little compost heap by the hoop house. She'd made it the I was young. The plastic sheeting was from the mainland; it had been stretched over the top of the boats during our trip. The hoops she created with her bare hands from copper piping she'd torn from the walls of two of the smaller buildings on the island. With her grip she had soldered them together, and then twisted them into semicircles and staked them into the dirt. I helped a little, as much as a mortal boy could, tugging the sheeting over the hoops and tying it to them.

"You're my little moron," she said as she sat in the dirt before the compost heap. The old her had returned. "You're so slow. You've mastered nothing of my art or science. I have to make everything easy for you, a little utopia just for you. Even now, I'm walking myself to my very grave because you'd probably spend two nights crying over me if I'd stayed in bed, and then you'd have to drag my carcass by the ankles to get me out here, if you even remembered what I told you—bury me in the compost heap. Your body rejects what I could have implanted in you, and your mind rejects what I could have taught you. I blame your father."

She turned away from me and looked out into the distance, over at where she knew the city she had left once stood. "I should blame myself," she said, contemplative again. "I selected his sperm, after all, but did it the old-fashioned way and let fortune take its chances with me.

"I'm dying now, son," she said. "Do you understand what I've been trying to do? Shall I whisper in your ear what I've been trying to do, or will it just confuse you? You're so easily confused, moromou."

M is for a lot of things. Moro is Greek for *baby*, and mou is *my*, the possessive pronoun. M is for my baby, and I was my mother's baby. But M is for more than that—I was Soteria's baby, but also her moron. In ancient Greek, *baby* was moron—thirty-five hundred years served to whittle off that final n-sound, but it preserved itself in the notion of someone being as stupid as a baby.

I was not confused though, and I told her so. I got on my knees next to her, and held her in my arms and stroked her hair. "I'll tell you," she told me, "I'll tell you what I've been doing..."

"You don't need to, Mother," I said. "I understand."

"Do you..." her voice was empty now, like a breeze that had already passed over us and into the Pacific. "Do you..."

"Yes. You love me. You've been so cruel to me these last days to make it easy for me, so I could bury you without crying, carry on without missing you so much," I explained, and I smiled.

And Mother looked at me and started to say my name. "N—" she began, but sticky pink phlegm left her lungs, drowning the vowel, and she passed onto the next world in my arms.

I buried her quickly, and left the compost undisturbed, and waited for years alone until the shimmering in the air and the coming of the glider.

11

It shames me to report that my first thought upon becoming lord of these isles was to think, What would the Master do?

Not only was it a shameful thought, but it was a foolish one. I know what the Master did—he left us somehow. I could only presume it was the washed-away men that triggered a long-gestating plan to make his escape, but that did not explain why he had abandoned little M. Could he not know that she and I, in our own ways, found these two men and rescued them?

What would the Master do...were he in full possession of the facts?

He would separate M from Francis and Stefano, of course. But were the Master here, his authority would not be dependent on the good humor of these two men, my new lieutenants with their blue eyes glaring at me like a quartet of cormorants.

I could not very well announce that my queen and I would be retiring to our royal chambers. M was looking up at me, stiff. Her expression was like the smiley face I painted on my favorite rock so as to have some company after my mother died. When the Master first arrived, I threw it into the sea.

"Well," I said. "I suppose we should have a feast!"

The men howled in glee, and we took the lighthouse as our own.

Neither the Master nor M ate much, and my lieutenants were only enthusiastic about food to feed the machines within that were regenerating their flesh, so what was available upstairs was uniformly excellent—food as aesthetic pleasure. I set M to work with an imperious pointed finger, and she obeyed robotically, clearly terrified. Francis joined her in cracking eggs, peeling root vegetables, and sautéing the garlic and onions I had paid just half a season ago as a tithe to my former master, but she did not relax into the work in the slightest. I helped myself to the Master's work chair—he was a big man, and it was practically a stiff-backed throne made of reclaimed wood—and tossed my legs over one armrest.

"Ah, there's something regal about you!" Stefano cried. He was drinking the dandelion cordial straight from the bottle. It was the only alcohol we could make here—potato mash and barley for a bit of vodka, plus the flowers, and there was even a lone and tiny lemon tree on the island. "You are a real king, my liege!" He bowed dramatically, spilling some of the booze. I licked my lips despite myself.

"Give it here!" I held out my hand in what I thought was a kingly manner, and took care not to say please. I decided that I might say thank you, but only if I approved of the taste of the liqueur, which the Master had never once shared with me.

Stefano smiled at me and bowed—a bit too low, perhaps mockingly—and proffered the canteen. I took a swig, and the liqueur was an explosion of grass and sugar and medicine in my mouth. It was a struggle not to spit it out, not to twist up my face like a baby refusing food. I let it fall down my throat, and it burned sweetly.

I'd never been intoxicated, though I'd read about it, saw it on my shows. I knew it shouldn't be instant, but the booze ran through my body so quickly I shivered. I didn't want to have anymore, but I was the king now, so I took a second swig, and a smaller third one, before tossing the canteen back. "Very good!" I bellowed. "And how goes the preparations for the repast!"

"Excellent, Lord...uh?" Francis called from across the room.

"Kalivas!"

"Mr. Kalivas," said M.

"That's me," I said.

"You're a Mister?" asked Stefano. "Is that all?"

Whatever M called me, I craved to be. The boys wanted more from me, so I told them, "It's enough for me, but I'll eat first."

"You're the one who needs to," Stefano told me. He gestured toward the table in the corner. M had set places, and in the middle of the table was a roasted bird—whole and stuffed with fish from the smell of it, which was excellent—and a chaotic seaweed salad spilling from the edges of a platter.

"All hail King Kalivas!" Francis called out. He saluted with the glass in his right hand. And his left arm snaked around M's waist. She looked up at him, and smiled. My internal organs about fell out of me and splattered against the floor, painting my ankles in blood and shit. I about swooned, and what appetite I had vanished. My stomach filled with wet sand. All things horrible and somatic; my body was willing itself dead.

Somehow, I got to my chair. I stammered my thanks and bid them all to sit with me and share the meal. It was a party—we were all friends as I was a generous and beneficent leader—and they all complied. M sat next to me! But she was also seated next to Francis. I had Stefano on my right.

"So, O King of mine, tell us your plans for these islands," he said, prodding me. He poured some of the liqueur from the canteen into my water glass. There was no saliva in my mouth, I was a desert. M met my gaze, but only politely. Her hands were under the table. Was she gripping Francis's hand in her own already, squeezing affectionately, thumbs stroking and twiddling?

Yes. She was, yes! Yes, she was, I knew it.

"I plan to marry," I said. "You'll be my queen as you said, won't you?"

"Yes, of course I will, Mister Kalivas," M said. I suppose I'd hoped lightning would strike her spine, as it had mine, that she would fall into an abyss of hopelessness, that the green in her eyes would leech into her skin for me. But no, these beings, they can control their natural physical responses to bad news, to threats, to misery. She was a portrait hanging in a gallery, an immortal beauty.

"Will I be your best man?" asked Francis. "Shall I hustle little M over to you, pay her father the dowry should he return?"

"No, let me be your best man. I'm your first lieutenant. And besides, Ferdy's hands on ol' Mandy here isn't what you're after now, is it? You might find his fingerprints where you least expect 'em."

I saw a way to defuse the taunting. "Ah yes, speaking of—where is your father, Miss?" I ignored the boys, trained my gaze on M. "Where is...the Prosperous One? You must know."

"The Prosperous One!" M said. "You're eating his food at his table!"

"It's mine now, recall." I wanted to add, *And you are my queen!* and snatch her free hand, but M was a strong one, and another humiliation, nor a set of broken fingers, I could not bear. "And I've had my lieutenant search the immediate islands for him. Not a trace!"

"Perhaps you need better lieutenants then," M said, waspish. She didn't let go of Francis's hand though.

"Perhaps we'll have another freak storm and be able to repopulate the entire area," Stefano said. "More women. You'd like that, eh, my liege? You could be more than a king; we'll make you a fez, you can be the sultan!"

"I'm satisfied with the number of women in my domain at present. One queen is sufficient," I said to him, as regally as I could. Then I turned to M. "But surely our wedding will need a father's blessing, Miss. So where is he?"

"Francis, let's go back to my room," M said suddenly. "Make love to me...again."

The room swam before my eyes. Could she be lying to make me feel terrible? No, she was telling the truth to make me feel even worse.

Francis looked at me. "Would you mind terribly? We won't be too loud." He was a handsome thing, now that his flesh had repaired itself. A man of wax! Taller than me, his voice deeper and more euphonious. He was wearing one of the Master's garments, but it fit as if it were tailored for him.

"Eat first," I said. And I carved the bird, slapped meat into their dishes, scooped up the salad with my hands, and served it with a whip of my wrists. "I'm sure you two can be a little patient. Group dining at a table is the cornerstone of any modern civilization."

"Well, I don't normally eat—"

"Yes, Francis. Exactly," I said.

They could have risen up against me, the two of them. The three of them! But instead they acquiesced and ate the meal with me. Indeed, all three of them seemed to have stronger appetites than I. I shepherded them into changing subjects to their own status as my subjects.

"I cannot have you all living here while I suffer in my hut," I said between bites.

"It's a lovely hut, though," said Stefano. "I suppose I'd be happy in it."

"And Mister Francis will live with you," I said. "M, of course can keep her room here, as befits a queen."

"And you'll stay in Father's room!" M said.

"Your father owned all these rooms, all these islands," I said. "He made that much very clear to me. I'd say that I bear the scars of his pronouncements, but he was able to torture me without leaving a mark." I kept my gaze trained upon her. "A common family trait, I'd say." She pushed some fish into her mouth to have some excuse not to offer a rejoinder.

"My mother, Soteria Kaliva, brought me here as a child. She was toiling here until her death, though the nature of her project was unknown to me. I was too young to understand. I propose that the three of you, with your enormous, hot-wired brains, help me determine what her project was. It'll pass the time between dinner parties such as this one."

"So, no dinner parties every evening?" Stefano asked.

"Lovely as this is, no," I said.

"You've not talked about your mother much before now, Mister Kalivas," M said.

"I wasn't king before now," I said. "She spent a lot of time in the radio room. She was like you all, you know."

"What are we all like?" Francis asked.

"What's the term? Inhuman?" I smiled at him, regally.

"Your mother was inhuman? Mister Kalivas!" M said. "What would that make you?"

M was much smarter than the two cretins we had fished out of the waters. I couldn't back out of what I'd said, so I just pushed forward. "Human. That was her choice for me. She was posthuman, looked at what your ilk had wrought, and decided to spare me."

"Ah, so if you were to be thrown into the ocean, you would...actually die?" Francis asked.

"That is why you're going to be living in the hut, not here in the lighthouse, Francis," I said.

"That's Mandy's name for me, not yours."

"Now now, friend—he is our king," said Stefano.

"And my first command is to determine what my mother was up to," I reminded them. I'd always presumed that the Master had come of his own free will, in search of my mother, whom he very occasionally referenced once he understood who I was. Once, the Master even went digging through the compost heap, though my mother's body had been utterly consumed, and not a trace of either her flesh or her technology remained.

I briefly described some of what I remembered, the little things she would say to me, what she would shout that I could hear through the radio room's windows while I played outside. The two men looked at one another quizzically, their mouths working, gazes trying to communicate something. Finally, it was Stefano who spoke.

"You know who would know?" he said, gesturing across the table at Francis. "His father would."

Francis started, "Well—y-yes, but...he would...I would..."

"You would?" M asked him.

"I...used to would."

"Used to would," I repeated. M looked concerned, interested, but not at all suddenly disillusioned. That feeling was for me.

She spoke. "Poor Francis wasn't quite what he once was."

"Ah," I said. "Is this about...the voices?"

Francis nodded, chastened. Stefano shrugged.

"I frequently hear my mother's voice," I said. "Moreso in the old days, before the arrival of...the Prosperous One."

"What would she tell you?" Francis asked.

"Mostly, it was an echo of what she'd tell me when she yet lived—that I should grow up and be a palikari." The three of them peered at me like seals. "A good man. A strong young lad. A warrior, but also just a male who achieved something, who is forthright."

"That's pretty vague," Francis said.

"Many words are fundamentally untranslatable," M said. "My father says so."

"But did he say so just now?" Stefano asked her.

"No..."

"You just have a hang-up!" Stefano said. He held an index finger aloft, then tilted it my way. I would have sliced it off his hand were I a real king, right then and there. Who dares jab an accusing digit at their lord? "Mommy issues! We're not talking about daddy issues."

"Oh good," I said. I looked over at M. She was beautiful as ever, but I couldn't help but twist her plain, perhaps slightly confused, expression into a rictus of pleasure. I imagined her on her hands and knees, taking it from Francis, his thighs slapping against her ass like in a pornography. Making love.

"What we're talking about is constant collective communication," Stefano said. "What one knows, we all know. Were you in our court, back on the mainland, you wouldn't have to explain the word pally-carrie to us. When you said it, we'd know it."

"Even if we couldn't articulate it," Francis said. "We would get some sense, a body-sense. What you felt when you thought the word we'd feel. So we'd know what you meant even if you couldn't properly define the word."

"Imagine the intimacy one could experience on the mainland, Mister Kalivas!" M said.

"You two must be at loose ends here," I told my lieutenants. "Having to do all your thinking yourselves, no father to tell you what is so and what is not." I looked upon M. "And you too, Miss. Without your father, look at you!"

"What about me, Mister Kalivas?" There was a sharp rock in her throat.

"Don't you hear the voice of your father in your head?"

"I don't."

"Not now or not ever?" Stefano interrupted me as I was about to speak.

"Not ever," M said. "Before a few days ago, I never heard my father's voice in my head. I have no idea what any of you could mean by that. I was with him almost absolutely all the time, except for occasional visits to the shore, or to Mister Kalivas. I heard his voice in my ears, when he spoke to me."

"But now that he's gone, you hear nothing? No voice

castigating you for your bad behavior?" Francis asked. Even he was unnerved. "Or prodding you on to achieve and do well?"

"I've never engaged in any bad behavior. As far as achievement..." she shrugged.

"What was the last thing your father said to you before he took his leave?" I asked.

"He didn't tell me where he was going if that's what you're asking, Mister Kalivas."

"That's not what I'm asking!" I sputtered. I squeezed the meat in my hands between my fingers like I was strangling the life out of the beast it had once been. "Willful child! What was the last thing he said?!"

Stefano and Francis sat in their chairs like dead things, stiffer than they were when we'd found them. M straightened her mouth and said plainly, "He told me that I was growing into an utterly delightful young woman and wished me a good night, and sweet dreams."

"I see—"

"And that he loved me very much."

My veins, my heart, filled with silt. I imagined the Master's voice, saying I love you very much, words I'd never heard in that order from him, or from anyone. My mother hadn't been the emotional type.

Francis touched M. Touched her! "That sounds like," he said, his voice tentative, yet clearly practiced, "he was saying good-bye, and farewell. As though he had no intention of returning. And he is right. You are an utterly delightful young woman, and of course he loved you very much." He shared a quick look with me, then shifted his attention back to M, who remained stoic. "Who couldn't love you? Am I right, my liege?"

"You are right indeed, Stefano," I said. "But I don't think the Prosperous One is gone forever."

"So you're ruling until his return?" asked Francis. That jack o'lantern smile. I wanted to punch it in, but his face would just reknit itself. Even his teeth, like stalagmites and stalactites, would reform eventually.

"These islands have been mine since I was a child. My mother created a life for me here. But as you can see," I said, gesturing at our food, "I'm generous to a fault. All are welcome, so long as they understand what these islands are, and whom they are for."

"They're for the birds!" M said with a cackle. "It's true, you know. In the final human days, Los Farallones were a bird sanctuary."

"That explains all the shit on the rocks," said Francis.

"Oh Francis, be kind," M admonished him gently. Then she touched him.

"That sounds like something I'd say," Stefano said.

"'Oh Francis, be kind?'" asked Francis.

"Complaining about shit on the rocks!"

"I see you have acclimated to your new name," I told Francis. He shrugged helplessly. M beamed at him.

"If rocks splattered with bird droppings are a problem, perhaps I should order a general muster of labor among my subjects to scrub them clean. At least on this island. Is it a public health concern?"

"Maybe for you it is," said Stefano. Then he quickly added, "as our king!"

These three—the entire public of my little kingdom in the sea—of course have no health concerns. They might even live long enough to see the birds of these islands evolve into new species before existential boredom kills them, or they kill one another through either stupidity or high emotion.

"Before we all traveled down the tangent of birds and their shitting, I was attempting to articulate a single fact,"

I said. "These islands were abandoned by men for decades. My mother reclaimed them, for me. Neither the birds nor their excrement have ever harmed me, which is more than you can say, Stefano. Or you, Francis."

"Call him Ferdy," said M. "Francis is my name for him."

"Call me Ferdy," said Francis. "At least when we're all together." He smiled winningly at M. They were about to touch one another again, in front of me.

"Well Ferdy, I think it is time we say our good-nights," I said. The food was nothing but dirt in my mouth now. Some king I was, some ruler of these immortals. They thought they could mock me and my birthright. "Do you two men require sleep, or have you regenerated sufficiently? You may share the hut."

"Oh, we're in excellent shape," said Stefano. "I mean, I'm in excellent shape. Who knows about..." he waved his hand toward his comrade. "Francisco. Ferdinand. Whatever you like to call him."

"Francis!" said M. "Did you know, Mister Kalivas, that on the mainland, people are rarely ever addressed by name? They just know one another. And it's not because the population there is so low; there have been just the three of us, you and I and my father, for so long, as Father and I are constantly calling you 'Kalivas,' aren't we?"

I made to stand up, hoping the men would take the hint and emulate me. M continued. "You may deny it, but it's because you're my servant. How odd, that you were here when my father arrived and agreed to become our servant, and now you're the king!" Neither of the men moved from their chairs.

"I thought perhaps I'd get a tour of the facilities," Stefano said. "It's hardly fair. Uhm, Francis has already seen them, haven't you?"

"Oh yes. It's a good time, touring the facilities," said Francis, his gaze steadily on M.

"In the morning, perhaps. You two, to the hut."

"Would you like to come with us, Miss?" Stefano asked M, obviously on behalf of Francis.

"She stays here," I said too quickly, embarrassingly. I hadn't even thought of a reason, dubious or not, why she should stay behind, in the lighthouse, alone with me.

"Do I?" M asked, her tone arch instead of guileless. And after just having said that she never heard the voice of her father in her head.

"You do."

"Why's that, my Lord?" asked Francis.

"She has a royal duty..." I said. "To help me sleep. To sing me to sleep."

The three of them laughed, Stefano loudest. "Good one, My Lord!"

"Do you like my voice so much, Mister Kalivas?" M asked.

"I think I should also stay, if you wish Mandy to remain here," Francis said. "After all—"

I raised my hand, but that wasn't what stopped him, mid-thought. There was a shimmering, and then a huge stroke of lightning and simultaneous thunder. Enormous, as though the table's centerpiece revealed itself to be a grenade.

The rain came in huge sheets a moment later. This was no natural storm. They all knew it too, perhaps thanks to their heightened senses, or sheer reasoning—a storm wouldn't spontaneously form over these little pimple-like rocks in the broad black flesh of the ocean. They would have felt the pressure dropping, smelt the ozone on the wind for hours before the weather hit.

"After all, you two might be safer in my hut," I said.

"And what about you, my king?" Stefano asked. He took the carafe of dandelion liqueur and emptied it down his throat.

"As you say, I am king. And even if I were to hide, my own bed would be a poor place for it."

These poor immortal geniuses were so stupid.

12

Once, when M was just beginning to come into her own as a human being—she could talk, walk, express desires, have fits and then regain control over herself, manipulate both me and her father with tears and the ridiculous if compelling ad infinitum rhetoric of a child—the Master came to me in my hut. The moon was new.

He shook me awake and without further greeting, with his hands still upon my shoulder, with the technology in his palms warming even as I blinked twice, three times, to bring his face into focus.

"Tell me of your mother," he demanded of me. "Or I'll...I'll..." I'd never known the Master to be at a loss for words. His eyes were wild instead of their normal placid blue. The weather in his mind was bad, I could tell. I was young, but I could tell.

"My mother treated me better than this," I told him. "Sit, please." The Master did so, right on the corner of my bed. He didn't apologize, but he did pat my knee through my blanket.

"Tell me, how was she, as a mother?" he asked me.

"She was the greatest mother to have ever lived," I said. I gestured about the dark room. I knew he could see it as well now as I could in the daytime. "What other mother could swim the Bay and create a life for me, one safe from the machinations of the mainlanders?"

"You wound me, Kalivas," the Master said. "Are you insinuating that my own travel here with my daughter is less of a feat than that of your mother, or that I am a mainlander and brought the machinations of my people to your doorstep?"

"You woke me for this?" The Master seemed maudlin, where a moment ago he had bordered on manic. The dandelion cordial and potato moonshine would never affect him so. His body would not allow it, though I wondered now if he specifically attenuated something in his gut or brain in order to will himself drunk.

If so, a possible weakness!

The Master glanced away, into the gloom of my dome home. "I would like to have known your mother. I was an admirer, from afar. She was frequently discussed in the media in the days just before the world turned on its head."

"What would you say to her were she here now?"

He snapped his head back at me. "Why do you ask me that?! 'Were she here now,' indeed!"

"Master..."

"Kalivas, this is a hard life, one of exile. How could your mother ever stand it?"

On the screens, I'd often see someone like the Master was now, head hung low as if all the anger had leaked out of their lungs. On the screens, the other character would often put their hand on the sad person's shoulder, and say something along the lines of "I know how you feel,

Kendall." I wanted to, that was the way people interacted with one another, but somehow I understood that in this case, it would be a bad idea, and the moment would end with a sizzling red palm print on my chest or face.

"She...had her problems," I said, finally. "She wasn't perfect."

"Was she not?" He tilted his face my way, peered at me out of the corner of his eye. That royal brow, rising.

Of course Mother was perfect, except for her illness and death and her abandonment of me, vulnerable and half-educated, but the Master was hanging on by a reed. I had to think of something. "No, she was not...uh, this is difficult to discuss, you must understand."

"You may tell me anything, Kalivas," the Master said. Perhaps he was now hoping for something juicy, even scandalous.

"She..." there was a shimmer in the air. "She did her best. But in truth, she came here for her own sake, and I was essentially ballast. She was disappointed that I was unable to match her genius, or even understand her work to the extent that her graduate assistants did."

"My girl wants a rabbit, Kalivas," the Master said.

"A what? Oh yes, with the ears!"

"Yes," he said. "With the ears."

"Was it her favorite food? Perhaps we can—"

"She wants a rabbit as a pet!" he snapped. Then, calm again. "I told her there were none to be had here, that there were no land animals at all, just the birds and the beasts of the sea, and she suggested I manufacture one out of a newborn seal."

"And that is not possible."

The Master glared at me for a long moment. His eyes were wet. "Indeed," he said, finally. "What have I done?"

"I've wondered that myself," I said. I was less careful

now than I'd learned to be at the Master's hands. There was something frail about him. His daughter was his weakness. "You'll live for centuries, at least. How can you occupy your time here for that span? And you'll continue to allow your daughter to age..."

"Will I?" the Master asked.

"If you wish her to attain the age of reason and put away childish fantasies of pet rabbits, you will."

"Mmm."

Then he spoke again. "Of course, she'll grow up to want other, less childish, things. What did your mother do for you? Did she discuss it at all, you maturing, having needs?"

"She left me the pornographies, if that is what you mean," I said.

"That will not do for my daughter," the Master said, his voice like the tide coming in all at once. For a wild moment, I imagined the unimaginable—that M would grow up, that the Master would have us marry and couple. Then he planted his palm on my chest, pushed me back onto my bed, and burned me. I hissed and writhed under him, but wouldn't give the Master the satisfaction of a howl.

He stood, withdrawing his hand. "I am sorry, Kalivas. I appear to have made a significant miscalculation. It may take some time to set the world aright. I hope I'll have your full cooperation."

Naturally, he would. I was powerless against him, against both of them. The Master could torture me with a thought, and M would one day be able to break my heart with a word.

13

The Master's bed was no better than my own. Perhaps a little worse, if anything. It was his body that was better, that could adjust to the hardness of the plank under the thin blanket, that could control its temperature sufficiently to never feel a chill. I was the lord of these islands now, and was patently miserable. The Master's own robes were my only extra covering. Oh, for my hut! My mother had cared for me, after all.

Soon enough, M was at the door. She opened it without knocking, entered without a word, and stood over me, hands on her hips. The light spilled out from the doorway, obscuring her face but not her posture.

"Are you comfortable, Mister Kalivas? I certainly hope you are. A monarch needs his royal rest," she told me.

"What's the matter, girl?" I asked, perhaps with more grumbling than was prudent.

"I'm not a dog from one of your children's shows. There's nobody trapped down a well," she said. "But there is something the matter! You sent my man away! I found Francis—he's mine!"

"I sent them both away," I said. "This is my kingdom. I make the sleeping arrangements. And frankly—" I sat up in bed and thumped it with a fist "—I did them a favor. Your father mocks my Greek name, calls me a 'hut-dweller,' but this is more Spartan than I can tolerate."

"Maybe I want them both," she snapped at me. "They're more fun together. They chitter and peer at one another like little birds. And they're both cute and I've heard there are things three people can do as well as two."

"Go back to your room." My voice was low, calm. I hoped to sound like the Master, to make her comply.

"I want to be where they are!" M said. "And I want you to hold a tarp over me as I walk to the hut so I won't be so muddy."

"It must be three in the morning, and it's still raining," I said. "An unnatural rain, don't you agree? It's not the season for thunder. When was the last time you heard a storm like this? Zeus and Hera, throwing plates at one another!"

"Talking about the weather? Boring! Your speech is a cure for hearing."

"If you want to go to them, go," I said. "But I'm not going to deliver you unto those washed-away men. Be wet and bedraggled, go to them half-drowned, your curls copper-snakes smeared against that lovely brow. See if they'll take you in. See if they're not too busy with one another to make room for a girl."

M laughed. "You want me to stay here with you, don't you! As if! You were probably thrilled when I woke you just now."

"Until you opened your mouth!"

"You can't stop me. I'll walk in the dark, backward, the wind on my back. See if I don't slip and fall into the abyss!"

"You might crack your head open, but I think you'll be okay. The boys won't notice any difference." M winced at that. My eyes were adjusting to the light. Her face had gone horrified and sorrowed and scared all at once. She could break my heart with a word; I could tear her soul in half with a sentence. There was a shimmering in the air. M shifted on her feet, as if straining to hear something. The room filled with a blue light, then was swallowed by the roaring dark. Direct hit!

Neither of us said anything, nothing that I could hear anyway. My hands had found their way to my ears somehow, and my eyes were suddenly salted, stinging.

There was another bang, different than thunder. It smacked suddenly rather than rolled across the sky.

"Something hit the storm panes," I told M, but she already knew and was moving faster than I could to the stairs, to the tower. I didn't take a moment to slip on my tunic, which was a mistake. Instead I gathered the Master's robes, which I'd been using as blankets, about my body.

By the time I was up the stairs, the wind and rain had stopped. The ruins of a man, leaking blood and other fluids, lay crumpled on the floor amidst a choppy sea of broken glass. M stared down at him, incredulous. Then she turned her gaze to the empty space where the pane had once been, and there stood the Master. Dry.

"Has there been a coup?" he asked as his gaze took me in. "A second coup?" I fell into a swoon.

14

When I awoke, the Master was still cross, though less so with me than with the entity with whom he occasionally communicates. I was so perplexed by the Master's sagging shoulders and muttering that I did not realize at first that my head wasn't resting on the folded-up robes of my master, but on M's lap.

She looked at me and her face was warm, almost giddy. Her lips twitched. "Mr. Kalivas, hello. You were unconscious for quite a while. You soiled yourself. Father told me to clean you, but I summoned Francis and had him do it. The man my father threw through the window is Francis's father. He was on the ship too. My father found him five leagues under the sea, or perhaps it was twenty-thousand fathoms. They fought for days, but my father prevailed, though it was a near thing. Nearer than Father would have liked—after all, Mister Anthony was already weakened, already waterlogged, and still he nearly subdued my father."

"Urhm...I see." My throat and my lips were so dry, as

if the greater fraction of the water that made up me had been boiled away.

"How exhilarating," M said. She squeezed my shoulder. I wished she would choose to run her fingers through my hair, but no. I tried to raise my head, but found it difficult.

"Rest, Mister Kalivas," M said. "My father took great offense at your recent political maneuvers. It's best you not further remind him of your crimes by sitting up, or groaning, or shitting yourself again."

"What's he doing?" I croaked out. M had a small cup of water next to her; she tilted my head up and poured some down my throat.

"He's talking to the spirits, of course. You sound terrible."

"What if I said there's no such thing as spirits."

"Then who is my father talking to?"

"He told you he talks to spirits when you were young?"

"The genius loci, my father calls it," M said. "And he is surely talking to something, as every time he does, whatever he was working on or planning comes to fruition. I'd hate to be the topic of his conversation now. I've never seen him so furious."

"Where are the boys?"

"They are...in the compost heap," M said.

"I'm surprised I'm not there with them," I said.

M shrugged at that. "It wouldn't help you. Father would just toss your carcass into the sea. You're the only one around here who can die, Mister Kalivas."

The dryness was gone; somehow my body summoned a gallon of sweat and instantly secreted it. I could die. I was going to die the moment the Master turned his attention back to me. No wonder M was being so kind—she'd be rid of me soon enough, and could have a life with Francis, or Stefano, or even Mister Anthony. Perhaps that was the torture the Master had planned for them. Smiles and compassion from M, then incineration and slow, painful resurrection, ad infinitum, until the sun grew large and blood red and destroyed the atmosphere.

To be perfectly honest, it sounded glorious. Much better than simply snapping out of existence, and the cosmos continuing to expand into infinity, my own life in the tiniest speck of time unworthy of notice. Why only die once, and quickly?

The Master approached. Whatever the theme of the conversation he'd just finished with the air, it did not conclude to his satisfaction.

"Kalivas, Lord of these isles," he said through his nose, in imitation of me. The Master was a tall man with a broad chest. He had the gray hair and slight jowls of an older man, but the technology embeds would not let him decline. I, not quite half-starved, a life spent just only protected from the elements, was smaller, my spine practically the letter C, hair everywhere, and one thick brow. His impression was uncanny, probably augmented by his exquisite control of his voice box. It stung.

"I'm Lord of the Lap at the moment, Master," I told him, my own voice as deep as I could make it. "Will you burn me upon it, and scorch your daughter's thighs?" With that, my head hit the floor as M quickly sat up.

"How dare you!" Her voice was like her father's now, and it reverberated throughout the rounded lantern room. "I show one moment of human kindness, yes, human kindness, and I get repaid with disgusting talk. Father, I don't care what your plans are for this one now."

"I'm sorry—"

"Shut up! Don't you dare talk to me! After all I've done for you!"

I reached out to him, and my hand went through him. The Master was not in my presence after all, but had projected a seeming of himself, the way the lighthouse's great lamp could hint at a golden walking path to the mainland when fired on a foggy night. I startled, pulled back my hand, and rather than gazing at the miracle before me, examined my knuckles to see if the image had burned off any hairs.

The Master was grinning at this. Perhaps I needed not to fear another radioactive bombardment. There was precious little left of me to boil, and he wasn't truly in the room anyway. "Yes, you've done so much for me," I said, fashioning a grin of my own. "A back to burp, someone to eat the food I gather. Someone to talk to, but never deeply, while the two of you discuss me as though I'm not even here—that is, when you're not talking to someone who isn't even here."

"Can you believe him?" M asked her father, gesturing at me like I was a piece of driftwood, absurdly shaped. Then she looked back down at me. "I owe you nothing, Mister Kalivas. We're neighbors. Do you know that word, neighbors? Nothing more."

"Invaders, usurpers, settlers, colonizers, I know those words as well. These islands were my mother's; they were mine," I said. I was feeling bold. "You didn't raise a new rock from the depths and plant yourself upon it. You didn't lease from me, or buy, or do anything but raise your hand and stake your claim."

"Oh, my daughter doesn't speak for me," the Master said, his tone amused. "Perhaps I shouldn't use the term neighbor either. I agree with you that whatever my family is to you, neighborly is not it."

M made to speak again, but the Master raised his palm, and she snapped shut like a clam. "However, perhaps we can still yet become neighborly. Imagine my despair when just a few days ago, my old enemies appeared just off the shore in a cutter capable of withstanding the most vicious of natural storms. It took all my might to repel them, and then, left weakened, the devil Mister Anthony attacked me outright. Two days in the briny drink, and then two to heal, only to discover that my daughter has taken up with my rival's spawn, and my servant—"

"Servant, is it?"

"Would you prefer 'slave'?"

I held my tongue. No, he held my tongue. The Master was deciding how I spoke, if I spoke. I could almost taste his salty hand in my mouth, his fingers' grip.

"Ah yes, two days in the briny drink! Two days to heal. And then, further incursions, betrayals on my very doorstep, warming my very bed. My girl, betrothed; my servant, wearing my clothing. The world has turned upside down!"

"Father," said M, "I must marry sometime. You married, didn't you? You raised a baby, a real one, me! Why shouldn't I have the same chance?" She looked down at me. "I'm sorry I called you neighbor, Mister Kalivas. You were more than that to me; the very model of child-rearing, I must say. I remember four women, or perhaps they were automatons, or just four waldo arms, back on the mainland, but you were my true nurse-maid, Mister Kalivas." She side-eyed her father. "You were."

"And not by my command, either," said the Master. His gambit nearly worked. It was all I could do to keep from leaping to my feet, embracing them both, acknowledging that yes I loved M, and that perhaps the Master wasn't so bad either, and that we could have normal lives, just the three of us, as we always have. M would get over her fascination with Francis in time, and could retain her youth, or couple with me, or simply age herself into eventual oblivion if she ever truly grew bored.

But I managed to keep my bones from jumping out of my skin. And I recalled that my arms would just flow through the Master anyway, whether I wished to embrace him or strangle him. O, for a coin to flip!

"What is my command is this. A costume ball! Una gran pachanga for my family, my enemies. You too can have a final hurrah with your new friends and playthings, and I will show Mister Anthony who truly holds the power in these lands, and bring him to heel." Again, I should have risen, if only to spare myself the Master's gaze from down his prominent hawk-like nose. "I have two heels, after all. Why should I not have two men at them?"

He had nothing else to say to me, and not even a gesture to commit. In an eyeblink, he was gone. I slid off M's little lap, and without a word—for what did I have to say to her?—I began the walk back to my hut. A low and throaty peel of thunder followed me.

15

"A quaint device," my mother had called it, that communication device that creates shimmers in the air. I've since learned that among the humans of Saint Francis and the lands beyond, quaint was a complimentary term, meaning pleasing. On the other side of the world, in what was once called the United Kingdom, quaint means old-fashioned, unsuitable, pre-modern. Soteria had been a bit of an Anglophile. I never saw many shimmers, and this upset Soteria to no end as she was in constant communication with the device, and I was too dumb to perceive it, but she came to her own end before ever clarifying what was so quaint about the device. I couldn't even see the device, which I understood to be near if not part of the lighthouse, and given the straits of my childhood, I had no true understanding of either meaning of the word quaint. I still don't. The word appears only rarely in my pornographies. I do believe that people once found lighthouses quaint, as they are both charming and old-fashioned.

My mother had interacted with the quaint device and

whatever entity it sympathized with through speech, through signs and gestures. After her passing, the shimmering in the air appeared only rarely, no matter what I did, until the arrival of the Master.

And now the air shimmered again, all around me, profoundly, like rain, as I walked to my hut. Was the entity attempting to communicate with me? Was the Master indisposed after his battle, leaving the unseen creature lonely or hungry for gossip? Bah, only in my dreams does the Master sleep. In my waking life, he is always awake. I felt a bit dizzy, so I stripped off my tunic and lurched onto my bed as soon as I entered my home. A soothing-sounding rain came.

And then, a knock at the door.

"Come in, Mister Anthony," I called out.

"How did you know it was me?" the man's voice returned.

"I've never before experienced someone knocking on my door," I said. "Everyone I've ever met just walks in as they please. So, you must be someone new to this land and its ways, and old enough to remember an era of manners as well." And while I knew how to answer a door, how to step aside and say, "Won't you please come in," and gesture with your left hand as they do in the pornographies, my utterance had exhausted me, so I could barely croak out a final ¡Bienvenido!

He walked in, looked at me, and gasped. I looked at him and gasped. He would need days in the compost heap, but what was shocking was his face. It appeared to be intact, even noble, yet familiar, but in the dark of the room I could see that his cheeks and brows were emitting rather than reflecting light—it was a projection along the lines of the Master's. What horrors lay beyond the illusion I remembered from the lighthouse? He did not, or could not, cloak the rest of his body in the fairy light. Golden ulnae and tibiae peeked out between curtains of blackened meat; his fingers were gone entirely. Mister Anthony's face, why he gasped at me, it took me a moment to understand—he was distressed by my nudity, perhaps because his own genitals had been visibly burnt off by the palm of the Master.

"Are you the one that has been making the air shimmer so restively?" I asked him.

"Cover yourself," he said.

"Your man Stefano took my blanket to wear as a cape," I said.

"Then use your hand."

"Is this meant to be a pornography?"

"What?"

"What?"

He was silent for a moment and glanced around my hut. "This is it, then?"

"The lighthouse is more impressive. People find it quaint," I said.

"Which people?" he asked.

"I'm sure many," I said. "Mr. Anthony, I had a day of anguish and abjection. I was also king, and now here I am, naked upon a bed stripped of its clothes, with a headache. Why have you decided to bedevil me instead of burying yourself in the compost to heal?"

"I need your assistance in—"

"If it's in 'overthrowing the Master' forget it, I've had a bellyful."

"You dare interrupt me!" He raised the stump of his arm, about to bring the burning pain. There was a shimmering in the air. I cringed reflexively and whimpered like a seal pup in the teeth of its father.

He lowered his arm. "Ah, the 'Master,' is it? The Prosperous One has done a number on you. That's what he does, after all. Do you know who I am?"

My body was alive again, fear and relief awakening me. "You look a bit like the Master, but everyone I've ever met does, at least somewhat," I admitted. "The same wan face, the same brows, the same gaze, and when you all smile, it is as though you have seen animals smile and seek to imitate them. And your hair, you could be Miranda's father. If this image was once true to life."

"It is. You'll see. And yes, her father...or uncle." Anthony said. "There used to be many more people in the world, Kalivas—"

"How do you know my name...what I am called?" I asked. Another wizard; no wonder Anthony reminded me of the Master.

"Your virtual HQR psychographic code, of course." He read my stare well and tried, "I read it in a book," instead.

"Who wrote the book?"

"Your master, I suppose." Anthony stepped into the middle of my hut and sat cross-legged, making himself at home. "I doubt your mother called you Kalivas, after all. And he likes books. That's why he's known as 'the Prosperous One,' really. It's a name he gave himself; he hacked his own HQR. And hacked minds too. His true nickname, and every true nickname has to be bequeathed by others, was 'the Bookkeeper.'"

"Like...a bookkeeper?" I'd encountered the word in various media, and I understood there was some sense in which the bookkeeper was in charge of money, or at least numbers, but I couldn't describe what they truly had been or why anyone would either want to be one or wish to be around one. When Anthony raised a glowing eyebrow at me, I explained all my ignorance to him, and he nodded.

"Yes, like a bookkeeper. No collector of antiquarian tomes was he. He kept score, the fool. Every conversation was a transaction, every assemblage of matter a bit of property, every relationship a competition. He turned a perfect existence into a dreary one," Anthony said.

"I know the feeling," I said.

I left it at that. Anthony also let the seconds pass without saying anything.

"Perhaps you are wondering why I am here," he said, finally.

"The rain?"

"No, I need your assistance."

"Ah, yes." I let the sound of rain against the roof work like punctuation.

"You may be thinking why I might need your assistance," Anthony said. "And no, it is not to overthrow the Prosperous One. He can have this place."

"Yes," I said. "He clearly can."

"I wish to free you from your state."

"Then you don't require my assistance; you believe I require yours."

"I believe in mutually beneficial arrangements. I wish you to travel back to the mainland with me. Your life here, in the wild, as a man who could only depend on the strength of his limbs and the speed of his wits, is intriguing. My people need your example. I admit that many of my people are forgetting how to live. They knew enough to send my brother, the Bookkeeper, into exile years ago, but they grow complacent and foolish."

"I believe I've noticed."

"Come with me, back to civilization."

"Oh, you think you have a civilization going over on the mainland, do you?"

He smiled. "Well, I did knock on the door."

"What would the mutually beneficial part of this arrangement be? Do I get my blanket back?" I smiled at him, but my smile was that of an animal. Face to shining face, I knew my teeth would glow with menace.

"I can...improve you," Anthony said. He held up an arm. "Pardon me. I realize that might sound condescending, and given my current appearance, you might even say I could hardly throw stones. Ha ha, both literally and figuratively. But, Kalivas, I can improve you. Do you understand?"

I didn't say a thing. He smelled like a brush fire.

"Kalivas, you will not ever have to die," he explained to me. "You could have the power of your mother, but without what brought her down. The plague has been eradicated. All that we are is your birthright as well, and all that you are right now is what we need to be again."

"I..."

Anthony didn't wait. He stepped forward in a flash, leaned down, and kissed me. The man still had a tongue, though it was dry, like the zwieback I remembered from my childhood. And it tingled, a 9-volt battery pressed against my tongue. The aches of the day faded, my ears unclogged. I could see in the dark now, better than an animal.

"That's just the beginning," he said as he separated his face from mine. A thin strand of saliva hung between us, then fell away. "A taste. A taste for me as well! But you'll see, soon. With new eyes, you'll see, and hear, the AI. It's real, and it is all around us. It had just been kept from you. I can save you, Kalivas."

"What a queer little narrative you present to justify your own actions."

"Get up," he said. He was all business now, like the Master. "You need to come with me, to dig up my son and my valet."

"Do it yourself," I told him, then wiped my mouth with my forearm. I could count the individual hairs as I scraped them across my lips.

"I can't," he said, holding up to stumpy hands. The nubs of his fingers were only beginning to swell, though I could see the faintest outline, an aura. "Plus, you'll want to see what's outside. It's a beautiful night, a fateful night."

16

I had thought Anthony meant the stars. Out here, away from the lights of the city, the doom of night is speckled liberally with stars, the squirt of the milky way, and annual meteor showers. The sight of the stars was my true birthright, not anything Anthony was selling.

Or so I thought, until I followed him outside.

The air was full of fireflies.

"Fireflies," Anthony snorted, somehow, despite his holographic nose. "How do you even know what fireflies are? They've never existed in this region, even before the plagues and the great heating."

"I've seen them in my pornographies," I said.

"They have lightning bugs in vintage porn now?"

"The animated ones often begin with some pleasant sunrise, or the coming of the crepuscular twilight," I said.

"Ah yes," said Anthony, as if he'd watched a few examples of the peculiar and foreign genre. With a wiggle of his shoulders, the fireflies began to alight upon him.

"Nanodrones," he said. "Far smaller than even the

dots of light my kiss granted you the gift to see. They swim in the air of the world. It's how we live, how we communicate, how we...do virtually everything. There are almost enough for everyone in the world."

"Almost?" I asked.

"They are not distributed equally," he said.

"Ah, the Bookkeeper." I was pleased with myself for swallowing the phrase the Master. "But the fireflies seem to like you well enough."

"And yet, I still need to eat, rest in compost, do a little nude sunbathing now and again. Have you ever seen my brother or niece lolling about on one of yonder rocks under the high noon sun, Kalivas?"

"Well..." I said, "no." But the pornography practically filmed itself in my mind as I spoke.

"Dig up my son," Anthony said. "My servant as well. I think your blanket is in there with them. The nanos will clean it off, I promise."

I got on my knees and began to dig. The night was warm, and the compost was steaming. As I moved the dirt and rotting vegetation away, I could see more fireflies burrowing through it, emerging out of it. They swirled about my fingers and wrists, keeping them from being scalded too heavily.

Was I one of them now? Did all it ever take was a kiss? Why did my mother never kiss me? She said that my body had rejected what she offered me, but there was never a kiss between us, not the sort of kiss that Anthony had...

A hand reached out and grabbed my wrist. I grabbed the arm's wrist with my other hand and pulled with all my might. Stefano slipped out easily, like a seal calf being birthed, and he was nearly as messy. My blanket was in tatters. The fireflies swarmed him. I squinted, blinked, and found that I could see past them after a fashion, to better examine Stefano's ruined face and limbs. Though still smeared with compost and dirt, it looked as though he'd been haphazardly skinned with a white-hot whip, and yet, with what was left of his lips, he smiled.

"Mister Ka..." he said. I shushed him and started digging for Ferdy, who was deeper underground. In my peripheral vision, the fireflies swarmed. Anthony was pushing Stefano with one foot, rolling him back and forth in the soil.

"Why are we even digging them up?" I demanded of Anthony. I was elbow-deep in the compost. I'd found Ferdy's head, but kept digging for a limb. "They'll regenerate faster underground. As would you, I don't mind saying. All of this could have waited till the morning. The morning of next Tuesday!"

"You keep track of the days?" Anthony asked, but he was mostly musing to himself and didn't care to hear any answer I might give. In fact, I do not keep track of the days. I'd just heard "next Tuesday" often in the media my mother left for me to consume. "You should be keeping track of the weather, Kalivas. A storm is coming. An unnatural one. Look up at the sky."

In the years before the Master arrived, I was quite the stargazer. The stars were scattered across the sky like shining white pebbles on the muddy shoreline. But since the arrival of that fateful glider, I looked only at the grass between my feet. Now, I turned my head to the sky. There were no stars high in the firmament, but a stream of fireflies was low against the gray slate. They were leaving the island, flying off Anthony and the boys, from the ground and the air about us, like eager seeds pushing themselves into the storm clouds.

"If the drones are leaving, that's all the more reason to keep your men in the compost, and for you to join them!"

I shouted. The wind was picking up, that's why I was shouting. I had no personal concern for these well-jerked, golden-wired half-men.

"A storm of the size the Bookkeeper is ordering up will wash half the island into the sea!" Anthony said. "The compost heap and everything in it will be food for fishes." Stefano was stirring and scooping compost into his mouth, snorting like a seal. Only a light sprinkling of fireflies flittered and flickered about Ferdy's head, but they illuminated the scene enough for me to find the crook of his right shoulder, and I was able to free him easily enough. The rain began to fall in great splattering drops, and waves swelled upon the nearby cliff.

"Drag him!" Anthony barked as he bent over to help Stefano to his feet. He had a pinky and a thumb on his pseudopod hands now and used them to get a grip on Stefano. Ferdy was light enough for me to carry upon my broad shoulders, but he felt cold and wet, like some whale calf that had washed ashore. But unlike that one happy morning when the ocean had delivered such a gift unto me, I was not feeling lucky as I followed Anthony back to my own hut.

The wind pummeled the walls of the hut, and the fireflies had not followed us inside. There was no place for me to lie down, not when three other men had helped themselves to my bed and my chair and the floor. I stood by the door with nothing to do but smell their filth and attempt conversation with Anthony, who was full of ideas about the storm and the Master.

"He seeks to kill us all," he was saying. "This is his revenge."

"Why would he do such a thing?" I asked. I felt like a child. "Who would wish to be king of mud and corpses?"

"If you could have killed him and his daughter,

wouldn't you have, to keep these islands for yourself?" Anthony asked.

Not M, no. I would never have harmed that one curl on her infant head. I would have fed her milk from fattened seals, taught her the language of my mother, raised her to be kind rather than imperious and haughty. There was a shimmer in the air.

"Kalivas..." Anthony said. "The door." There was a knock at the door. There may have been a prior knock moments before, but the sound of it would have been drowned in the wind. Who could it be, since nobody save Anthony had ever knocked? I turned to open the door, but the knob was already twisting though I'd locked it. M opened the door and stepped inside my hut and walked right past me and stepped over Stefano and ignored Anthony who sat in my chair as if it were a little throne, and with her two white and remarkably dry arms scooped up poor desiccated Ferdy and carried him away. She winked at me as she passed, then kicked the door shut behind her.

"My son..." Anthony croaked out. "Oh, Kalivas, what shall we do?"

"Where even is the Master?" I asked. "I saw not him, but just a seeming, a projection. He said he wished to throw a great party."

Anthony groaned at that news.

There was a shimmer in the air outside, visible through every window in my little hut. The storm doubled, tripled, in strength a moment later. The lights went out. If there were any firefly nanos in the room with us now, they were dead. Even the two men in the hut with me had stopped glowing, stopped moving, would not speak, even when I called out to them. Something fell to the floor. I imagined it was Anthony, taking to his knees.

17

The night was long, as there was no dawn. The storm had eaten the sun. My mother's architectural and engineering skills were exquisite, but the hut barely survived the unprecedented weather. The walls quaked and shifted like they were drapery, and water found its way in through cracks and fissures I'd never perceived before. Anthony spent the night kneeling in a puddle, absorbing the water and what nutrients there were through the palms of his hands. Stefano stayed on my bed, half-dead. I had little to do but stand in the dark, shivering. I slept on my feet, a few seconds at a time, dreaming of falling, pitching forward, catching myself. It was difficult to lean against any of the curved walls of the little geodesic dome, but if not for the shape, I am sure the three of us would have been crushed in a collapse. I dreamt, in snatches, of lightning striking the lighthouse, the ancient lens and lantern splitting from the tower, and of M and the Master, in flames, falling screaming into the sea.

When the rain stopped, the sky remained gray. The

whole of the islands were loud with the screeching of birds and the bellowing of seals, and with some other suite of noises as well. I walked outside, my feet sinking in the muddy grass, and headed toward the noise, and toward a singularly disgusting smell. My tongue tingled with a stain of metallic filth.

A tanker ship had run aground. There were multiple tears streaking across the hull, as she had pushed her way through the "devil's teeth" of the smaller islands and shoals, or, more likely, had been pushed through by the storm-churned waves. I glanced over my shoulder to see that the lighthouse still stood, but nobody was atop it, observing the scene.

As I got closer, I could see that the ship was far from a wreck. Spider-like machines were scrambling over the deck and through the gashes, shifting boxes and packages about. A few shipping containers floated in the waters just offshore, but their doors were open, and they would sink soon enough.

"Mr. Kalivas!" I heard M's voice in my ear. One of the many skills this new breed of people have, thanks to my mother, or the fireflies, or both, but it was one she almost never used. M was as lonely as I, and would always seek me out, tug on my fingers as a child, slap me on the shoulder as a young woman. Not anymore, however.

"Look, among the wreckage!" she made my ears vibrate. And down in the water I spotted her in a skiff, rowing past some of the spidery machines. She let go of an oar and waved to me when she spotted me spotting her, and then returned to her rowing. "It's incredible! My father has brought us supplies for the party. This ship is full of wonders."

This was not my first tanker ship. When I was a child, I'd sit upon a high rock and wait for days, sometimes weeks, to see one or another pass by on the way to or from the Bay. I'd wave my arms and howl, to no avail. As I grew and my mother weakened before finally passing, the number of ships declined, along with the world population. Even signaling with fire did nothing. Only now did I understand that the ships had likely been uncrewed across the span of my whole life; there was never anybody aboard to communicate with. The spidery automata I watched skittering about now were uncanny—no front or back, no head or even a pair, or a dozen lights for "eyes." They didn't look like animals because there were no animals to look at them. Even the seabird swarms, who love to alight on any surface, kept clear of the wreck.

"Was the great tempest your father's doing, then?" I asked.

"Of course," M said. "What did you expect him to do—'hack the Gibson' to bring the ship over?" She laughed at her own joke, and didn't explain it. I didn't ask.

"What's aboard?"

"A veritable potpourri to be sure. What they used to call capital goods; fruit and beef, furniture. Father says we can use the containers themselves to build new homes. Teak floors!"

"And what of the earlier storm, the one that brought the washed-away men to our shores..."

"And Ferdy into my heart, you mean?" M giggled. "Father's work? No, or not really. The first storm was mostly dumb luck. Father's work is beautiful and terrible to behold."

I thought back to the condition of the men I'd dug out of the compost the evening before. "Indeed."

"Mr. Kalivas..." M started. "I have a request to make of you." From the sleeve of her tunic she removed a rolled-up piece of paper, the first paper I'd seen in years. There hadn't been a notebook on the island at all, so far as I knew, and the leaf was surely not torn from one of the Master's tomes. It had a yellowish taint to it and was lined. She handed it to me and said nothing else.

I unrolled the paper and looked. On the page was expertly drawn in pencil a diagram of a boat. It took me a moment to realize that the boat was composed of the roof of my hut as the vessel's hull, and elements of my hoop house as rigging, mast, and sail.

"I would like to leave this place," M said softly. "With Ferdy." That addition was like a tack to my heart.

"I..."

"Do you understand, Mister Kalivas?"

"Your father can summon storms."

"My father can summon...a storm, but it takes much out of him," she said. "It would be a long while before he could ever do it again."

"He could track—"

"No," she said. "That is one thing he could not track. It would take nothing more to build it than the simplest of tools; it need only last one trip, a mere nine and a quarter leagues. Nothing aboard attached to the genius loci. We'd be beyond Father's grasp."

"I wouldn't be."

She gave me a serious look, eyes gray like the cliffside. I half-expected a flight of birds to wheel over from a nearby hill and shit all over me.

"And..." I said. "What about the voices these new men hear? I presume..." I waved my hand in the air, trying to replicate the shimmer I'd see. It wouldn't do to tell M of my kiss with Anthony, and how I saw the fireflies that coated the world.

"I pulled the receiver from Ferdy's brain before the neuronic link regenerated," M said as casually as she would tell me that she wanted her eggs scrambled, not hard-boiled.

"What did he think about that?"

"Mostly with his unconscious, I imagine," she said. "He squeaked."

"What about your own brain?"

"I'm a daughter to a father, Mister Kalivas," M said. "Can you imagine the terror a father would face peering into the mind of a girl he raised alone on a rock in the sea?"

"Not alone, Miss Mir—"

"Without a mother, I mean!" she snapped. She'd never raised her voice to me that way before. "And anyway, especially now, my thoughts, my recent memories, would make Father blush, if his cheeks have grown back by now. You must build the craft now, Mister Kalivas, before the party!"

"I-I should build it?" I sputtered. "It is bad enough you want the roof over my head and the only way I have vegetables, but you expect me to do all the work as well? Should I wade into the sea and push the little boat for you?"

"But Mister Kalivas, you're so handy!" M said. "You've always done the work around here. What would we have ever done without you?"

"What will your father do to me!"

M gave me that serious look again. "Whatever he does to you won't be any different whether you assist me and Ferdy. The party is a celebration of my father's victory. The only difference is whether Ferdy and I will suffer alongside you, or whether you'll help us escape."

"Your father would never hurt..." I started to say, but then I understood what M meant. The Master would torture Ferdy as he had so often tortured me, and that would serve to bring grief to his poor daughter.

"All three of us could go?"

"Would that were true, Mister Kalivas," M said. "You wouldn't get along on the mainland. You'd be a zoo animal, a novelty, a media spectacle. I imagine you'd be tempted to hang yourself, and for a free-range man such as yourself, a hanging is a unidirectional trip. And that's if you'd survive the trip. We're not simply going to sail to San Francisco to be blown to smithereens by some other rival of my father who'll hope to hurt him by hurting me. You coming along would mean we'd need to carry water, as you cannot drink from the sea. You need to eat." She looked me up and down. "We just chose to eat, you know."

I did know.

"There's a cut in the world," she explained. "In the time of my great-great-grandparents, when everyone was like you, an army of men worked together to slice the continent in half. A narrow canal—do you know what a canal is? We're going to sail down to it, cross the canal, and put a whole other ocean between us and the nonsense of civilization. We'll find someplace as nice as this, I hope."

I snorted. This place had been nice, but lonely. Now it was as full of bags of technology and arrogance that walked like men, and an utter misery. I was human, a free-range being of blood and meat, like a bird or a seal, and thus didn't rate evacuation.

"I know about the fireflies," I said after a long silence. Silence between me and M, that is. The birds were carrying on as usual.

"That's nice. I hope to see some when we sail up the East Coast."

"I mean...the nanos. How they coat the world. The source of your..." the next word slid out of my throat embarrassingly easily—"superiority."

"Oh," M said. "Oh ho! Yes, well, those that aren't killed by the tech, your mother's tech, benefit greatly, that's for sure." There was a shimmer in the air. "Mr. Kalivas, I must go. Will you help me? I know it must sound absurd, me being a superior and all..." She chuckled at that. I loved her tinkling laugh, but this time it sounded simply unpleasant. M squeezed my shoulder. I felt the coldness of the little silver implant coin in her palm more intensely than the warmth of her fingers. "Help me, Mister Kalivas. You're my only hope." She laughed again, but I didn't get it.

The spidery drones, limbs laden with goods and technologies freed from torn-open shipping containers, began to clamber up the cliffside. How long would it take for the wrecked ship to sink beneath the waves, I wondered. It too was a quaint device, half-impressive, half-garbage.

18

I was not going to render myself homeless nor starve myself, not for M's sake. However, pulling the roof off my little hut under the pretense of doing so seemed like a good way to get Stefano and Anthony to leave. Surely, there wouldn't be a third storm over the course of a single week, and at night I could look up and imagine that the stars were the incredible fireflies that had once again become invisible to me.

The dome was cleverly designed and modular. The exterior was self-cleaning, just like the floor inside, so there was no need for preliminaries such as scraping off accumulated bird shit or wind-blown sand. First, I removed several solar panels, rolled them up, and sent them sliding down the curved side of the hut, then I got to work on undoing the seals around the polycarbonate hexagon at the very top of the structure. That was trickier work, and I banged around and cursed sufficiently that Stefano heard me and walked outside.

"What ho, Kalivas!" he called out. "Were you locked

out? All you need to do is knock! I'm feeling much better. I can work a doorknob again."

The panel finally came undone, and I flung it over my shoulder, aiming blindly at Stefano. I heard the soft thud of the panel hitting the ground and an imperious snort. "I know!" I shouted down to him, but without turning my head to face him. I peered down into my home. No Anthony. "Where is your father?"

"Preparing for war!"

"He didn't strike me as much of a warrior," I said as I undid another panel.

"His specialty is retreat," said Stefano.

"Oh?" I was going to throw the panel over my shoulder, but instead I just gripped the edges. "Will he be...?"

"He will be building a boat!" said Stefano. "Can you imagine such a thing? His thought is to uproot your little hoop house, turn it upside down, and just drift away. He called it war in the hope of inspiring me to help, but if I am honest, I prefer terra firma and your remarkable little hut.

"Which you are currently dismantling?" Stefano affected the ancient California accent, which transformed statements into interrogatives.

"I need my hoop house to live. I cannot sustain myself on eggs and seal blubber alone. My mother told me to eat green leafy vegetables and potatoes every day, and I carry out her wishes. Nor can I just shove any pile of filth into my mouth and turn it into perfect posthuman flesh," I said. "Not like some people."

"After a fashion..." Stefano said philosophically, "Anthony also needs the hoop house in order to live. Your master will surely slay him otherwise. He came very close, just days ago."

"So, your lot can die?" I tossed the panel in my hands onto the ground near Stefano's feet.

Stefano waved his hand. "There are levels of living and dying, you see. It's hard to explain, you just have to experience them. The levels, I mean. The sleepless nights, the lightless sleeps in the nutrient muck, the choice of wrinkles or blushing cheeks for the younger crowd. The old men are old forever, I'm afraid. Your mother's wizardry came too late for them."

"You know of my mother," I said. I removed another panel and tossed it forcefully. It's always windy on the islands, so the panel sailed over Stefano's head, landing an inconvenient distance away from the others I'd detached.

"She's famous. The best thing since pasteurized milk!"

"I've never had any pasteurized milk."

"You only notice the difference between it and raw milk from not shitting yourself!" he crowed. Then more to himself than to me, he said, "Ha ha, shitting yourself. Imagine such a thing..."

I knew the fireflies, the nanodrones, were all around me, though I could no longer perceive them. I tried crossing my eyes, but nothing. Then, a great inhalation—could I gulp some down into my stomach and then absorb a few into my bloodstream? Surely, I would have done so by now after a lifetime in this world. For a moment I daydreamed about somehow tricking Stefano into giving me a kiss. Bah, I should have tried something with M earlier; a sturdy ship for an enlightening kiss! But now, she probably would have just boiled the water out of my skin cells. There was a shimmer in the air. The Master often muttered to something; I knew now that it was the fireflies. Perhaps they were surveilling me. I whispered to them, or to Master, or to the spirit of my mother—whomever might have been listening.

Stop Anthony from taking apart my hoop house. Then I added, *as I am nothing but a cringing slave to these people, to these devices I did not until some days ago comprehend. Please, my Lord.*

19

Well, the hoop house was indeed taken apart, but not by Mister Anthony. The same tentacular drones that had arrived on the islands in the ship scrambled up the hills and captured the man, then disassembled the hoop house themselves, then carted away the piping, the plastic covers, the planters. They piled unripe potatoes in pyramids and bound my spinach and vlita in shaggy bunches of leaves. Anthony went with them silently, almost solemnly, though he had been seized by the wrists and the ankles and hoisted aloft, to be marched off to...

The Master, I presumed.

Nobody would be building an escape vessel any time soon, but as Stefano ran after Anthony, calling his name, I achieved my proximate goal of driving them both out of my home. There are no wheelbarrows on the island, so I'd have to go home first and find or contrive some sort of bag to carry the crops. Could I bury the vegetables to preserve them somehow, or was I doomed to eat as much as I could before they grew rotten, and then just wilt like a leaf myself? I shoved vlita into my pockets and selected the best-looking potatoes to hold in my arms and headed home. The sun was setting, and I knew the stars would be especially beautiful as they are every night after a storm.

Most of the birds, and there are tens of thousands, fall silent when darkness comes, though there are still many creatures squawking each evening. This night was noisier than usual, perhaps because drones were crawling all over and between the islands. The stars were majestic enough, a great pale stripe across the ebon sky, but I was restive. I turned on one of my favorite pornographies, one that was more than a century old, to drown out the cacophony of the night.

The pornography was in black and white, almost as rich as the night sky above me, and dealt with the machinations of half-naked supernatural beings. Women descended into a virgin wood on beams of moonlight; a little servant boy crawled forth from the ground; a powerful man much like the Master, wearing a sequined costume that glimmered as if strung with fireflies, commands the servant to do his bidding. There was a fellow named Nick cursed with a donkey's head—I admit that with him I could identify, even more completely than little Puck. Two men and two women are compelled to fall in love with one another, and even the donkey-headed man receives some affection. Finally, the various players retire to an amazing castle of the sort I thought the Master would compel me to build with my bare hands, and...

There was a knock at my door. Nobody knocks on my door, except for Anthony, who had been captured by the Master. I turned my head away from my screen, and out of the corner of my eye I saw it. An eyeless spidery drone crawling along the hole I'd put in my roof.

I rolled off my bed as it sprung at me, landed on my

knees, and gripped two corners of the bed sheet. The drone was a small one, the size of an ambitious seagull. There was another knock at the door, this one emphatic. I threw my sheet over the drone and quickly folded it up.

The door flew open and through it leapt a second drone. With an underhand swing of the drone in the blanket, I knocked the second drone back outside, then followed it. If more drones were coming, it was better to be outside where I could run in any direction than be trapped in the little round box of my hut.

The drone flew at me again and again, with the most satisfying echoing thwack I'd ever heard, much less produced, I again made contact and sent it skittering away. Long years of downing birds by tossing rocks at formations of them translated well to this game of swing and strike. These drones were smaller than the ones that had earlier seized Mister Anthony—and other than the one I was smacking with, which was unstable and scrabbling away in my sheet, and I swung the sheet overhead to keep the drone too busy to right itself and escape—and only the drone I was striking a third time now, and a fourth, was after me. Did the Master underestimate me? Was I, a dumb animal lying in bed and watching a screen, so easy to seize and drag off to some night of torture?

"Guess not!" I shouted aloud, as if the Master could hear me, and indeed he probably could, but he surely could not hear the thoughts that had proceeded my exclamation. If he could, I hoped he was blushing now. If not, my overhand swing at the scuttling drone, which took its legs out from under it and gave me the chance to kick it against an outcropping of rock, would stain his cheeks red.

With the death of its comrade, the drone I'd wrapped in my sheet and utilized as a weapon stopped wiggling quite so much. Was it afraid, or was it hoping I'd peek inside the bundle and have the chance to rip off my nose and gouge out my eyes? Perhaps it was waiting for yet more of its brothers to come over the hill and capture me. If I let the beast go, I would be surrendering my advantage. The sheet had several small tears in it now; if I tried to smash the drone within against a rock, it might split the sheet entirely and free the drone to renew its attacks.

I saw only one option—holding the sheet closed tightly, I tossed the drone over my shoulder and started walking toward the Master's lighthouse, which is where the drones were meant to drag me in the first place. But I'd walk into the great party under my own power, partake of the foods and drink of the gods, and look my immortal Master right in the eye and demand the return of my hoop house.

Lord, what a fool this mortal is!

20

I remembered, as I trudged over the dark hills, that the Master's gran pachanga was meant to be a costume party. This was an unfair and distressing realization, as my mother never provided me with sufficient surplus fabric and craft-items with which to make a costume. I knew from my pornographies that dressing inappropriately for a party meant instant and inevitable social disaster, though for the most part what I have seen were people showing up in costume for a party that wasn't such an affair. Was social ostracization commutative—was it as bad to be the only person to show up unmasked at a masked ball as the reverse?

"Little drone on my back, if you stop squirming, I'll let you out. There's no need for conflict. I am sure you can sense that I am going to where you were told to bring me. We can walk together to the Master, if you like."

On my back, the drone stopped squirming.

"Excellent," I said to it. "I will let you go, but if you wish to accompany me any further, rather than simply beaten against a rock like an octopus and kicked into the sea, you must cooperate."

The drone remained still. Silence equals consent, at least in matters of state, so I let go of the sheet. The drone scuttled free of it, and did not run away and did not reach out to entangle my ankles, so I explained what we must do.

I was the only man on the island to have a beard; even the Master was clean-shaven despite his age and power. Pornographies had taught me that wise men, aged rulers, and wizards often sported facial hair, but the Prosperous One and Anthony had forsaken this look. The two younger men preferred thin mustaches that looked much like caterpillars. I had only ever rarely let my gaze drift toward the Master's visage, as this was his implicit demand, and I only had eyes for M.

The drone detached one of its smaller tentacles, and I utilized the blade of one of its pincers to shave off some of my whiskers, which I then plastered with a bit of mud to the front of the drone's orb body, or at least the section of it which was facing me. With the sticks it had collected and stripped of bark to reveal the wet white wood underneath, I fashioned as a crown by tying them to my head with a scrap of the sheet. I wrapped the tentacle around my wrist and palm, an approximation of the silvery circles the immortal interlopers sport on their hands. I tied the rest of the sheet around the drone's body—the sheet was soiled and torn, just as my tunic was, and it had been the same color, originally.

"There we are little drone," I said to it when I was done. "We are in costume. I am the Master, and you are Kalivas. Let's practice." I held out my right hand and the drone bent the joints of its remaining limbs and shivered a bit in an approximation of how I cowered and trembled before the wrath of the ol' Prosperous One.

"Convincing! We are sure to be a hit."

The lighthouse was fully illuminated, from outside and in. The lens had been removed in prelapsarian days, but several large drones were in the lantern room, glowing and spilling light of all colors down onto the small cement checkerboard platform where the party was being held. Elements of my hoop house had been turned into a sort of pool, the hoops first flattened and then extended on either end, and the sheeting restretched over them. The light was such that I could only see the five revelers in silhouette as they splashed about in some sort of viscous substance the consistency of an egg yolk.

The party ignored me, even when I got close enough to make out their activities, and their features. They were naked, all of them, oiled like wrestlers, the Master thin and wiry and burnt red and brown like the rusted metal of my hoop house, Anthony broad with a carpet of silvery back hair. He could have been a seal masturbating against a rock. The younger generation was all entangled, slipping and sliding and grabbing great handfuls of the yolk from the surface of the pool, or from one another's bodies, and swallowing it.

Naturally, my gaze settled on M, as her naked body was of the sort I'd never seen outside of my screen and its pornographies. Mats of hair were splattered against her armpits, the delta of her legs, and her shins, though the curls on her head were strong enough to hold their shape, though the liquid dripped off the ends. She sensed me watching her and stood up into a low squat to peer at me. The four men continued in their splashing about, Ferdy sliding some of the fluid into the crack of his buttocks, his member huge and swinging. I looked away, to the Master rubbing his bald spot, Stefano sucking his fingers clean, and Anthony sitting in the pool cross-legged and smacking the liquid with both palms.

"Hello," I said. I held aloft the arm I had decorated with the drone-coil. I looked down at the drone and told it to bow to its Master and to M, but it did not. "I am here for the party."

They continued to peer at me, the five of them, M glistening and sleek like a dolphin breaking the waves, the others mere rocks jutting out of the sea.

"I was led to understand this party would be a masque of some sort," I called out. "I apologize if I misunderstood. I've not been invited to many parties over the course of my life."

They stared at me, all but silently. They breathed, the fluid dripped from their skins and plopped into the pool.

The Master raised his hand, not to show me his fearsome, blazing palm, but just to point. He croaked without meaning, once. M grabbed two great handfuls of the glop at her feet, shoved it all into her mouth, and then smiled, letting some of the substance ooze out between her teeth. She inhaled deeply, grunted forth an exhalation, and then opened her mouth to speak.

"Grrruurghhgkklluugghhh!" She blinked stupidly—her eyes were so wide in her head I could see her blink even at a distance, then tried again. "Blaarghhuukkk!" The fluid spilled from her mouth as though it were vomit.

The three interlopers clapped their hands and hooted and pointed at me, and at her, and at one another. The Master turned to me, unsteady on his feet, nearly stumbling, and pointed too. He was somewhat more articulate. "Kalibuh. Ha!" He'd noticed the drone and smiled. Then M fell face-first into the pool and landed hard and the Master wobbled, then followed her down.

There was a shimmering in the air. It occurred to me that perhaps I was not in fact invited to the party; if anything, the drones were meant to delay my coming here, or perhaps even murder me outright. I was the only ape on these islands even capable of death. Had the Master overestimated my fragility? He'd certainly underestimated my intelligence.

I left them to their bathing and splashing and took a walk around. A long table had been set up and a feast laid out with foods I'd never seen in the flesh, and fleshy it was. A roast suckling pig, birds I knew to be a turkey and a peahen and a California condor, none of which can be counted among the native birds of these islands. And there were bottles of wine, true wine from the look and smell of it. I remembered grapes from my youth on the mainland and have ever missed them.

The larger drones, the type that had seized Anthony, had arranged themselves on the corners of the little plaza in a decorative fashion, their tentacles entwined and suggestive of movement or a bodily silhouette. I recognized an attempt at Niké of Samothrace, and Venus de Milo, and Diskobólos. The fourth was some sort of abstraction, a bit like a child's crib-hanging mobile writ large. All were far more interesting than the scene in the pool, which was reminiscent of The Ricotta Eaters. Other drones beyond the square shined lights across the party floor and even into the sky.

I noticed then that the night birds, and their squawking and shitting, were all gone. I could see some in the distance fluttering toward or over the smaller nearby islands, and when I returned my gaze to the sky directly overhead, that familiar shimmering in the air was present again.

I returned to the long table and took a seat, though

there were only five at the table. In the pool, the Master's party continued to splash and grunt and howl for a long while. If the food wasn't growing cold and the wine not growing warm, it was because of the marvelous silvery trays the victuals were presented on, and the buckets of ice —real, miraculous ice!—the uncorked wine bottles rested in. Surely, the bizarre anti-party the Master was hosting a few meters from the table would be over soon and real festivities would begin. Would they all come to the table naked and glistening; would M sit in Ferdy's lap?

My stomach growled. My personal drone stood where I'd left it, close to the pool. The night grew darker. The Master and the others settled down into the pool, lying in the slime, splashing and only occasionally quietly yelling. I could not see much over the rim of the pool, but when one of the Master's limbs would be flung into the air by his twitching, I could see that the flesh had regenerated. He looked baby pink.

Eventually, language returned. "K..." said the Master. "Kal..." spoke the Master. "Kalivas!" cried the Master. He got onto his knees, then extended to his full height. Though his brow and the tuft of hair on his chest were still white, his skin was without wrinkle or blemish. The others rose behind him, all fresh and clean.

"You..." He pointed a long finger at me. My hands shook in my lap, though the Master was not showing me his palm. It would only take a flick of the wrist. "You live! You...are sitting at my banquet table."

"I am," I said.

He stepped out of the pool and found his robes, which were folded neatly by the far side of the pool. The others slowly made their way out of the pool as well, Anthony helping Stefano to his feet, Ferdy and M embracing one another.

"Do you know, Kalivas," said the Master, "that one should not arrive at a party early?"

"No, how would I know such a thing?" I said.

The Master kept his gaze fixed upon me but did not otherwise respond as he walked to the table. The others stepped out of the pool and put on clothes. M had selected a white shift with lacy decorative details I'd never seen before. The interlopers put their old outfits back on, now entirely free of the mud and filth that the islands bring to all clothing.

It was Anthony who was the odd man out, the one who chose to stand because I'd taken a seat. Stefano even looked at him expectantly, waiting to be ordered to rise to allow the older man to sit. It was the sort of expression I knew well, from the inside, from wearing it myself for so many years. Instead, he just offered the Master a wry smile.

"I imagine you're wondering why you called everyone here," he said to the Master. Stefano laughed obligingly. Ferdy and M only had eyes for one another. "Your attempt to kill me and my men failed..." He glanced over at Ferdy. "Spectacularly."

"You're welcome for the turn in the rejuvenation bath," the Master said.

"And thank you for wrecking one of the ships under my purview and appropriating its cargo. The bath was quite invigorating after you assaulted me."

"And you're welcome...on this land to which you exiled me these many years ago," said the Master.

"Exile," said Anthony, the edge in his voice suggesting a question. "We gave you everything you needed."

I laughed at that. Both men turned to glare. Listening to their conversation was swiftly becoming thirsty work. I snatched a bottle of wine, a glass by the stem, and poured myself some. It was red, a red I knew from pornography to call it, and when it filled my mouth it felt as though the flavor filled every cell. I shuddered in my seat, spilling some of the wine on my lips and chin. Whatever this was, it was more powerful than the dandelion cordial I'd taught myself to make in my youth. I was emboldened. "Ha ha," I said, "this one—" I gestured with my cup to the Master "was utterly ill-prepared. I wait upon him hand and foot." Then I pointed at M. "This one too. Could they eat without me, live in a fine home without me, thrive without my compost? Would they even exist without the innumerable gifts of my mother?" I emptied my cup.

"What a remarkable fellow you are, Kalivas," said Anthony.

"Now that the ship is here, we don't need you, as a matter of fact, Mister Kalivas," Ferdy said.

Everyone glanced over at him.

"It's true! The baths are far more efficient than his dirt and filth. The drones can perform all the physical labor. The supplies can last us years. And now that we are here, we can establish trade ties with the mainland," he said, excitedly.

"And what would be your main expert, ol' chum?" asked Stefano. "Bird droppings? Vintage forks—six of them?"

"Tourism," Ferdy said. M gasped. Even the Master snickered. "Adventure tourism," he added.

"Kalivas, can you sing?" Stefano asked me. "Are you a contortionist? Can you juggle fire? If I give you two three-digit numbers and ask you to subtract them, could you mentally calculate the difference and stamp your foot that many times?"

"I..."

"What if the result was a negative number?" he said. "Tourism! Really, Ferdy, I know not who is denser. We were brought here by accident, these two were sent here against their will, and our native host, King Kalivas, well—"

"I quite like my home," said M. "We should carve the meat. I tire of sunbeams and rotten vegetation and protein glop and eggs and seal and fish. Think of what a treat it will be for Mister Kalivas. Please, Father."

The Master picked up a large knife and a long two-tined fork. He stood and pointed the knife at Stefano. "You were not brought here by accident," he said, and then he pricked the taut flesh of the pig with the fork and set about carving.

Ferdy startled in his chair. "What do you mean!"

Anthony explained, "He created the storm; we were the experiment. The storm that brought the supplies was the replication."

"So you meant to trap us under the sea, food for fishes forever then," said Ferdy.

The Master served M first, then Anthony, letting Ferdy's question hang in the air. There was a shimmer in it.

"You mastered the aerial system," said Anthony.

"I meant to bring you here," the Master said. "Whole of limb and mind. Well, mind at least." He gave Ferdy his plate of meat. "So that I might have my revenge upon you."

Nobody was eating their banquet. The pig smelled delectable. Perhaps better than the wine. It was as though I could taste it from a distance, tiny atomized aspects of it released by the carving somehow landing on my tongue. The Master did not carve me anything. He did nothing but hold his gaze on Anthony, who was looking at Ferdy, and next to him stiff and bone white, M.

Stefano looked at me. I looked at his plate. He slid it over. I took the meat up with my hands and consumed it noisily. It was still sizzling hot to the touch, but my work-tough hands were proof against it. My lips and tongue not so much—ah, if only the work I'd done these years had involved my tongue!—but three mouthfuls of chilled wine helped with that.

"I wonder if that was somehow poisoned," said Stefano quietly.

"Ha! Who could poison a god such as yourself?"

"Another god perhaps, Mister Kalivas," said M.

"Oh…" I said. The pork was delicious all the way down to my stomach. The only bothersome aspect of it was that several small morsels of it had become stuck between my teeth. An unfamiliar sensation, given my usual diet of eggs and the tenderest fish. "Well, I've surely already eaten enough to kill me if this feast is meant to kill all of you, so I may as well clean my plate." After several more seconds of watching me eat, M tucked into the meat her father had sliced for her.

"So, Master!" I said between bites. "You'll have your revenge on these new migrants, will you?" Did I have a plan? No. Was I in fear of my life? In that moment, no. I was curious, as curious as I was the moment I'd first laid eyes on the Master so many years ago. "Surely, bringing them here is no revenge. Your realm is a veritable utopia."

The Master detected my sarcasm but responded only by raising the temperature around me by five degrees or so. Or perhaps it was the wine warming my limbs. It was certainly loosening my tongue.

"I find," M said carefully, "that the quality of a place depends on its population." She had already cleaned her plate, but her wine glass was full. I so wanted to snatch it from her. I even had the opportunity as she glanced over at Ferdy. "Los Farallones was once a wild place, untamed and empty. But it is a utopia, Mister Kalivas. Now."

I still wanted to snatch the wine glass, but now only to dump its contents over her head. Instead I said, "As you like it."

"My revenge..." the Master said, "is beyond your understanding." His posture was oriented toward the table, but surely his remarks were meant for me. "This place was, for a long time, free from human habitation. This is why your mother chose it for her experiments. There is a machine here, radically distributed across the islands, that nobody could quite understand, even as we were able to harness some of its capabilities."

"The quaint device," I muttered into my cup.

"The what?" Stefano said.

The Master snapped his fingers, and before I could answer, Stefano and the drone statues began moving and creating noises. Metal against metal, gear tooth enmeshed in gear tooth, rotors spinning and stopping, appendages stomping and tapping the ground, their own central masses whipping through the air. It took a moment for my ears to adjust, and when they did, I understood the cacophony as a polyphony, a symphony. Music!

And with song came dance. The drones moved from the corners, and the smooth-spinning wheels and twisting tentacular limbs added to the soundscape even as they carried out the choreography. I was amazed; the others were impressed. Anthony nodded along, seemingly appreciating mostly the mathematical complexity of creating a movement pattern that would in turn generate music from the epiphenomena of the choreography. M and the younger men stood up from their chairs and began dancing as well, mimicking the machines and giggling and smiling as they swayed and hopped and grasped at one another. The movements weren't all that different from the splashing and groping in the pool, but there was a certain refined vigor to these dances; it was the seduction that comes after the fucking.

Anthony took up a glass of wine and sipped, then stepped onto the floor. He placed the glass upon his head and, with perfect balance, twirled. He crossed his legs, bent his knees and sunk low enough to smack the ground with first one palm, then the other. Then Anthony spun and was up again; he kicked out his left leg and slowly pulled it back.

I knew this family of dance from childhood, from the mainland. The zeibekiko. I was a child, on the border between infancy and memory, at a wedding. Some cousin of my mother's. I remembered almost nothing of it, except that the pants I wore were scratchy and the collar on my shirt stiff. There was soda pop in a plastic cup. And there was dancing to the wailing keen of a clarinet and the metallic tang of the bouzouki, most of the serpentine trains of men and women, looping and spiraling across the room.

In corners, smiling men would drink and then when the spirit struck them, take to their feet and dance, solo. Pairs and groups would make room, sometimes women would kneel and clap. The zeibekiko was a matter of pure expression so far as I could tell; there was no set choreography, and it hardly mattered how dexterous one was. A toddler loping about or an old man standing on his head or a young fellow clenching the corner of a small table between his teeth and lifting the whole thing up—these were all zeibekiko. So, my mother explained afterward on the long car ride home, up into the Oakland Hills. I fell asleep in the back seat and woke up the next morning in my bed, still in my blue suit jacket and pants.

Now, decades later, at another banquet table, watching another man perform, beating the drones with bursts of randomness, emergent glee. Now I could drink wine. Now I could dress as I liked, albeit so long as it was in one of the few ragged tunics I owned. Was Anthony even Greek, or was this all my mother's work after all? I had another question as well.

"Is this your revenge, Master?" I cried. The three younger people circled Anthony and clapped as he danced. M dropped to one knee and snapped her fingers, her thin arms stretched high, her sleeves swept down to expose her beautiful white elbows. Even the drones seemed to respond to Anthony's dance, but without gathering around him. They made their own circle, with the tallest drone, one that was all limbs and no wheels, in its center. That drone wrapped itself into slipknots and fell out of them, tumbled and soared. It was a competition, I realized, between machine and machine-man. Was the Master meant to be the judge? Was Anthony dancing for his life?

The drones stopped, abruptly, and the music with it. Anthony continued his dance, three limbs moving through the air, one foot pivoting, his son and his man and M clapping in time. Anthony leapt up and landed on his other foot, bowed low, and then plopped onto his bottom. His breathing was heavy, but he wasn't perspiring. For the men of his ilk, displays of fatigue were an affectation.

"Bravo!" I shouted! *"Evye! Oreia!"* I started clapping too, my big callused palms great noisemakers that filled the space. "What a show! What a dance! What wonderful revenge, Master!" I laughed and laughed, a forced ha ha ha cackle like an actor in a pornography. "And Mister Anthony, an inspired bit of footwork from you."

The Master smirked. "Kalivas here is correct. You were inspired," he said to Anthony.

"And was I right about your wonderful revenge, Master?" I asked, or the wine did. "Are you killing them with kindness? Ah, if only you'd ever sought revenge upon me." I took more pork for myself, tearing a chunk of meat right from the carcass.

"No," said Anthony.

"Not yet," said the Master.

"Mr. Kalivas," said M, "didn't you admire Anthony's dancing? We all did. He did better than the drones, despite the limitations of his limbs, lungs, and limberness."

"But not his libido!" said Ferdy.

"His life," said Stefano. "Drones can move at a greater array of angles, adopt more advanced postures, and perhaps even innovate as informed by their algorithms, but they lack life, they lack soul."

"How are your knees, Anthony?" asked the Master.

"I could use another dip in the pool, if I am being honest," said Anthony. "But the contest was not one of endurance."

"But endure you do," said the Master. "Endure you do. You have endured through the upheavals brought upon this world. You bring into the present some seeming of the past. Your life, because you know what it means to live as a human, a free-range human."

Everyone fell silent then, even me. I'd stopped chewing. In the distance, I could hear the nightbirds scream and caw, the waves crash upon the shores of both the island on which we sat and those smaller ones scattered about it. But all those sounds were distant.

"But..." continued the Master, "could the same be said for our progeny? For your fool Stefano? They were born into this world."

"I won," said Anthony. "I beat you at this party game."

"You won...round one," said the Master.

I was confused and said as much, "I'm sorry. Could..." I waved my hand, "could someone...this isn't what I expected parties to be like!"

The Master hiked a thumb at me but addressed everyone else. "See this specimen? Isn't he something?"

"He's something else," said M.

"What did you expect parties to be like?" asked Stefano.

"Less ominous, I suppose. More dancing, with more women. Were there none in the cargo hold of the ship? Flashing lights and bubbly wine spilling out of glasses. Those little—" I gestured at my neck, tracing a cross over my Adam's apple—"bowties. And then they're untied, either by a furious man or an amorous young girl. Perhaps some kind of parlor game to be played? That's what I expect parties to be like, and that is leaving aside the costume party I thought this one would be!"

"Maybe he's not something else after all," said Ferdy. I didn't understand him, truly, but the statement and the tone in which he said it—and his look at M, the information that somehow passed from his eyes to hers, with nary a shimmer in the air—was clearly an insult of some sort.

"We could call it a farewell party," said Anthony, "though whom exactly is leaving remains to be seen."

The Master spoke now, an edge in his voice. "Oh, I don't think so. We know who will leave and under which condition," he said to Anthony. And then he spoke to me, the longest utterance ever directed at me. "This is a costume party, Kalivas. What you witnessed before, that was what we are sans costume. Sans means 'without.'" I knew that but dared not interrupt. "Your mother never emerged from the compost, did she? She was human. You inherited her humanity. We inherited the fruits of her unfathomable genius. Immortality!"

"Wizardry!" said Anthony.

"Some inherited more than others," said Stefano. "Others lost more of their humanity than some."

"Lost humanity, eh?" I said. What a phrase! I imagined a long line of people, dressed in rags, marching two by two over the curve of the world, tiny continents and puddly oceans under their feet. Where were they going? Where had they been? "Are you all lost humans, then? I could direct you all to the sea, if you like."

They all ignored me. "Anthony, you came of age before the great change. Your man and your son, however, did not."

"Nor did your daughter, Miranda," said Anthony. He spoke plainly, but to devastating effect. Everyone stopped breathing, save myself. The Master was right —these people were immortal, not human, and didn't strictly need to breathe, at least not all the time. It was a pretension, just as performing fatigue was, and both pretensions had dropped. Anthony was on his feet, he swaggered and preened. M and her betrothed and Stefano were struck dumb and as still as the drones. Even the Master failed to respirate as he licked his lips.

"We're both so old, brother," said Anthony to the Master. "We were born and raised to be like..." he gestured to me! "So I passed the little test Soteria had built into the systems. I can dance better—"

"Not better," Ferdy interrupted.

"More humanely?" M asked. "Human-ly. What might the phrase for it even be? Ah, organically!"

"Better," Anthony repeated. "Danced better than your drones, even if they could supply the music they danced to, even if they could move in ways no man could ever move. That should be enough."

"You're practiced," said the Master.

"And neither my son nor my dogsbody are, but neither is your daughter," said Anthony.

"Is there to be more dancing?" I asked.

"Yes," said the Master. "Miranda, you are in love with Ferdinand?"

"I am!" She clutched Ferdy's arm. Ferdy turned to the Master and smiled widely, his face a broad full moon. When I was a child, I'd learned that once, long ago, the entire world was threatened by the existence of great city-destroying nuclear missiles. It seemed that every leading power had at least a few, and some countries had thousands of them buried deep underground, sizzling away. I wished I had one now, to blow up the moon.

"And you, Ferdinand?" Anthony asked.

"I am, Father" he said. "I love her very much."

Stefano looked between the older men, hopeful, but they did not ask him to weigh in on the topic of loving M. I too was resolutely ignored.

"A bit sudden, isn't it?" I asked. It wasn't the wine talking, though I was full of it. "You two just met."

"Don't you believe in love at first sight, Kalivas?" asked the Master, a wide, curved grin on his face. Oh, for two ballistic nuclear missiles to destroy the crescent moon upon his face.

"I do," I found myself saying. And it was true that in so many of the pornographies I watch, people often simply knock on the door of a mainland home, are invited inside, and immediately set to fucking, sometimes among company or a party, much unlike this dreary affair. "But surely it isn't common. Surely most people don't fall in love with the second man they've ever seen."

"I'm sorry, are we supposed to dance now?" Ferdy blurted out, obviously bemused by my musings, but M soothed him. "We can dance as we please—there's no supposed about it."

"Do you realize," Stefano said, "that if your dance doesn't have a particular human element, one judged entirely subjectively by our host here, he will take some dreadful revenge upon us all?"

"Not me," I said. "Exclude me out."

"Not me either," M said. "Right, Father?"

"What if the dreadful revenge is endless searing pain?" I asked, flashing my palm at her in imitation of the Master's discipline. "Wouldn't seeing the man you love in agony ruin you, turn you against your father? But then where would you be, without anyone but a weeping, screeching man-child, and a mild pater turned cold?"

"Well..." said M, her tongue twisting along her teeth and lips. I loved that she thought with the whole of her face. "We'll have to be sure to dance in the manner of humans. And I have a way of guaranteeing that we can." She turned to Ferdy and flashed him a half-moon smile. No nukes!

"Ferdinand, my sweet boy," she said, "will you marry me?"

Everything inside me exploded.

21

The years between the death of my mother and the arrival of the Master are a blur to me. I was left with devices that served me, few other resources except for what I could harvest from the birds and the bays, and utter ignorance of what the world beyond the Farallon Islands had become. The air never shimmered, though the wind blew constantly.

The pornographies were seemingly endless, and as I aged, they changed. More explicit, but also more thematically and emotionally complex. Fewer cartoons as well. I developed the habit of talking to the screen, which I knew from the screen itself was considered an eccentric habit on the mainland, but on the mainland everyone had one another to talk to. On the Farallons, none of the birds could be trained to talk in the manner of parrots, or at least I got bored trying before any of them learned to tell me, "Kalimera, Kalivas."

What would I say to the screens? The sexual material hardly needed my cheerleading, or my ignorant suggestions. The interstitial plots, which sometimes went on for hours, were prime shouting material, however. For years I repeated punchlines to jokes, then began anticipating them. "...what, and quit show business?" was a favorite of mine, though at the time I didn't understand what show business was supposed to be.

I masturbated along with the more explicit pornographies, performed the calisthenic and aerobic exercises of the clothed solo shows along with the boxers and the yogis, and most of all enjoyed the long pornographies featuring one man alone in the wilderness, or on a distant island, or via some miracle of technology in a tubular home floating in space or a strange planet with multiple moons. Eventually, almost all of these lonesome heroes found a companion animal friend, a woman, or a return to civilization.

But not me.

Which one was it? What was I watching when I discovered the truth about the wondrous technology my mother had bequeathed to me? The title hardly matters; what does is that the fellow on the screen who was attempting to start a fire was an utter fool. He had been driven away from his community and left alone. For a time he had a pair of spectacles and had used those to start fires, though after a long rain the ground under him gave way and the lenses shattered. After the rain, he limped to the mouth of a cave, gathered a few large sticks, set up a perimeter of rocks, and started rubbing a pair of the sticks together despite his filthy, damp hands and long stringy hair hanging from his head.

"You'll never start a fire that way," I said to the screen, disgusted. It was raining across the islands as well, so I was doubly piqued. "And if you managed it, your hair would burst into flame."

I'd seen the scene any number of times. Indeed, the

man soon realizes that he cannot start a fire and moves to the back of the cave to shiver in the blue darkness. Then, behind him, we see a pair of bestial eyes slide open. But this time, something different happened.

The man raised his gaze from his task, and looked out as though through the screen, at me. He tucked some of his hair behind his ears, and then ran his hands along the floor of the cave until he found some moss with which he wiped his hands. He took up the sticks again, then dropped them as the mountain lion in the rear of the cave leapt upon his back.

The rest of the narrative proceeded as I remembered. The change was shocking, but immaterial. The man ran from the beast and desperately scaled a tree. It seemed as though the lion would simply scamper up after him, but the man was able to kick at a weak branch and send it falling onto the animal. He slept among the leaves, then ate raw eggs for breakfast, just as I often did.

When I watched the same pornography again, he took my advice automatically. The scene had changed. The screen could hear me.

"There is a mountain lion in the rear of the cave!" I shouted. The man, a fool, rushed into the darkness as if to confirm that I was telling him the truth. The video ended three minutes later, after some screaming.

I learned that I could alter the outcomes of events in other pornographies as well, though rarely for the better. After long, I stopped even trying. "Reach for one of those knives and threaten him with it!" I said to a woman sitting naked on a kitchen countertop, her legs spread. The plumber was surprised, but they ended up engaging in intercourse anyway after he parried the blade with the handle of his plunger.

I was a simpleton. Though the stories obeyed my

commands, I could do little to influence the narratives, not if I wanted to keep the characters on my screen alive. I could only make them act stupider. Nor would the pornographies extend very far beyond their climaxes. No children birthed or families raised after copulation, no king spending long years navigating the politics of their realm for decades after ascending the throne, no cities rebuilt by honest and frugal statesmen after the destructive alien invaders had been driven off, no families reconsidering their rivalries after the double suicide of their children.

What could I do? Nudge. Send a pirate crew down to Davy Jones's locker, and then close my eyes and imagine it was my mattress drifting upon the calm cinematic sea, but only if those pirates had a few lines. The leading characters might take to the plank upon my command, but then some new force—another ship suddenly appearing despite the wide horizon, a captive breaking free from belowdecks, tentacles rising up from the deep—would interrupt the proceedings. I took to watching pornographies about pornography to better understand what I was seeing. I watched tales of men with cameras in their hands or strapped to their chests, looming over women; stories of shouting foreigners in jodhpurs and crops shouting into huge funnels. Action! Cut! Sometimes, the people in the screen looked through the glass at me, and seemed to address me, though I was still a child when I realized that they were communicating with some generic viewer.

None of them knew my name, until one did.

It was broad daylight and I was hardly even watching the screen. The islands get hot in the summer and the autumn, so hot even the birds quiet down, the water warms around one's ankles. Like an animal with a favorite ledge to crawl under, I was in the little home my mother had left me, scraping some mold out of the edges of the room. The substance from which my mother had synthesized the dome was remarkable, but fell short of miraculous, and the climate of the islands is relentless. The screen was on mostly for the music behind whatever drama was unspooling. The sharpened shell I was using as a tool slipped in my hand and cut my palm. I shouted, tossed the shell over my shoulder, and clutched at my bleeding hand. The shell clattered against the screen.

"Ow!" said a voice, male but high. He was a man of blacks and grays, in a rumpled outfit and a tiny hat. A popular fellow who had starred in many a pornography, I'd never heard him speak before. He was covering his nose with both of his hands.

"What the..." said the woman next to him, a blonde, I supposed, though her hair was silvery-white. She immediately clasped her hand over her mouth and turned to me, her eyes wide. But she did not seem to see me; instead she leaned over as if looking down at her off-screen feet, then craning her neck. She was looking for the shell.

She elbowed the man. He pulled his hands from his nose, which began spurting a comical amount of blood. He clasped his hands back over his nose, then saw me, then shook his fist at me, and out of his right nostril spewed more blood. The blonde quickly handed him a handkerchief. He took it and clamped it over his nose, then tipped his hat at the woman, and accidentally sprayed her with blood spouting from his right nostril. He got his hand back into place around his nose, but she grabbed her handkerchief back to wipe herself clean, and he spurted yet more blood.

He turned to me, and once again took both hands from his face to shake a pair of fists at me, and as his blood splattered against his side of the screen, he shouted my name and told me to never watch any of his films again. The woman gasped, and the screen went dark.

The mold could wait.

I restarted the film. The black blood obscured the screen. I picked the shell up from the floor and tapped it against the glass to no effect. I cleared my throat. The man in the little hat and baggy pants didn't have a name so far as I knew. His pornographies were largely without dialogue. Would calling him "little fellow" be appropriate? The screen was smaller than me—every male in it was a little fellow, and all the females were little women. I was a giant, striding the world, until the coming of the Master and the maturing of M.

"If anyone in there has a handkerchief," I said to the screen, "I'd appreciate the effort to keep the screen clean." Nothing happened. My cheeks burned. "I'm sorry I threw the shell." Perhaps my first-ever apology. I was a willful child, the natural son of the world's greatest sorceress. She died before I had anything truly to apologize for, and living alone for decades, I was the one owed an apology. "Please help me," I said.

A squeaking sound emanated from the speakers. In the very center of the screen, a dot of white appeared then expanded, looking just like an iris wipe typical of the most ancient of pornographies. It was the blonde woman, with the handkerchief. When the screen was clear and the scene restored, she made a show of holding the dripping black fabric by two fingers and walking it over to a man in uniform, with a broom, dustpan, and a wheeled trash can. She dropped it on the ground; he swept it up into the dustpan and then deposited it into the trash can. She stepped closer to the screen, crossed her arms across her chest, and puckered up her lips, not for a kiss, but in the twist that women in pornographies use when they are expecting some sort of response.

"Good," I said. She glared. "Thank you," I said. Her posture relaxed. "So you can hear me," I said. She nodded emphatically.

"Always?"

She took a deep breath and cleared her throat, as if unused to using her vocal cords. "Yes."

"Why have you never addressed me before?"

"I just got here," she said.

"Why has nobody in the screen ever addressed me before?"

She screwed up her face again, in a different way. The silent pornography people were always so visually expressive. "In the screen," she repeated. Not quite a question.

I reached out and touched the screen. Her gaze didn't turn to my fingertips, but she did perk up. "Ah, yes. That's right. That's the activation."

"When the shell hit the screen?" I asked.

"Yes. Now the system will communicate with you directly. Directly, as in you can direct us, and we can perceive you. Thus far, all we ever heard was a voice, first a child's, then an adult's, as an impulse, an intrusive thought compelling us to do this or that."

"But when I was a child, my mother told me never to touch the screen," I said. "And after she passed, I was afraid to ever do so. If I were to break it, I have no way of replacing it, and I am all alone in the world."

The woman smiled, wryly. "How sweeter than dandelion liqueur to have an obedient child," she said.

"What?"

"What?" she said.

That was unfair. I had much more reason to be confused than she. The pornography people had always had one another to talk to, and to engage in intercourse with, and it seemed that they always knew that one day they would be able to converse with me.

"It's about time you pressed the button," she said. "So, how can we help you?"

An excellent question, the answer to which I did not know how to articulate. I had everything I needed to survive, including a screen full of pornographies that didn't talk back. But I also had nothing at all. Los Farallones even lacked four seasons. I had forgotten when my birthday was, the taste of carbonated beverages, the smell of other people, the joy of spying on a single, quiet animal waiting in a driveway or sitting upon a branch.

Could the pornographies help? For a brief time, it was a novelty. When I was lonely, I'd ask someone to raise their head from between the thighs of another performer and initiate a conversation. Sometimes, they were happy to do so. Mostly, I was just confused. I'd never spent time with anyone, so I asked over and over what the screen people were doing—why did you become a spy, or a boxer? Why do you copulate with strangers, while in another narrative, it takes weeks for someone to get a smile or a kiss out of the object of one's affection? If you were in a room with two other people, how did anyone decide whom they should address first? How did you get one of them to be your confederate against the other, or at least keep the pair from teaming up against you?

With the birds, it was simple. Nine times out of ten, the larger ones were victorious in any exchange. On those rare tenth times, it was the smarter birds who won. The black ones, the cormorants, they could manipulate events in such a way as to claim the food of gulls and even the pelicans. There were more cormorants among the men and women of the screen than there were pelicans. Cleverness, audacity, cunning were the prized traits. Beastly men and large women were mostly objects of fun, dim-witted, childlike, quick to anger.

The screen people helped me to become clever. My vocabulary expanded, my daydreams thickened. The directions I gave to the screen people grew subtler, more complex. Their performances became more enjoyable to watch. The conversations remained fairly limited. Almost nobody seemed to know what lay beyond the windows in their rooms, and my one attempt to bring the screen outside to show a small child the ocean failed. The child, a young boy even younger than I was when I was brought to these islands, drew a picture of what he could see with his crayons. I was a boxy head over an oblong circle of a body, with sticks for limbs, and all around me thick black stripes. The landscape was beyond his perception, nor could he hear the waves or the birds or the wind. He laughed, through tears, when I asked if he could smell anything, or taste the salt of the sea on his tongue.

I learned much about humanity, or I thought I did, via the pornographies.

Then came the Master. He was like nobody I'd ever encountered before. He could not be negotiated with, nor confronted, nor ignored, nor seduced. I would have thought little M would be his weak spot, but instead she quickly became mine.

22

It doesn't rain much on the islands anymore, but I felt something tapping against my shoulder, the back of my head. I looked up from the crook of my arms, picked my head off the table. It was Stefano, poking me with his finger, and sprinkling a bit of water on me from a leaf he'd found somewhere. One of the drones loomed behind him, medical appendages newly deployed and ready to go. I'd not seen anything like it before, except on my screen.

"Ah, you're awake!" Stefano said. My head was throbbing, as if my brain were seeking to escape my skull. He leaned down and whispered in my ear, though the words were like waves crashing against the shore. "Poor form, Kalivas. One is supposed to fall into a drunken stupor during the reception, not before the wedding."

One of the organs other than my brain activated, and dumped something sharp and sudden, like a thousand wasp stings, into my bloodstream. I was awake. Sober. Virtually a blank. I could sit up straight, but that was all. Stefano, whom a moment ago I'd known, was a stranger to me; the drone was just a tree of a different hue, and the trees I knew not.

It took a moment for my brain to understand what my mind was seeing. M was wearing flowers in her hair, haphazardly arranged in a wreath. She clutched a small bouquet. Anthony had a ring held up between two fingers; it was a gaudy piece with a red gem. I could not recall if I'd seen him wearing it earlier, or if it had been manufactured somehow for the occasion.

The occasion, yes. The wedding. A wedding. I'd seen them in my pornographies, though I of course had never attended one. Who was M to marry? Ah yes, Francisco! Francis for short. No, that was also wrong, but at the same time right. What was that handsome fellow's name, and why did his waxen face make me want to chew the sweetmeats of the bones of his skull?

"Ferdy!" M's mouth and my mind said at once. Where was the Master to put a stop to this? I remembered everything now. All the players on a stage, pornographies so often end with orgasms, as do weddings.

Master! I wanted to cry out, though my pride made me choke on the word. I was humiliated anyway, as Mmmmuh! managed to spill forth from my lips, and that sounded very much like the sobriquet of the bride.

"Mister Kalivas, you're awake!" she said. They all turned to me now, even the drones. Even my drone, the one dressed like me. "My father is having one of his little fits. Would you be so kind as to give me away?"

Ferdy said, "Oh no, sweetness! He shouldn't give you away."

My headache had returned. I buried my head in my hands and groaned.

"He should be the one to marry you!"

I sat straight up again. Ferdy smiled, not at M, but at me.

"I'm sorry. I mean to say that you should be the one to marry us, Kalivas. You are king and lord of these isles. The power is surely invested in thee."

"He'll do no such thing!" cried the Master. "There is no such power invested in him." He was up above the scene, on the catwalk that wrapped around the lantern room of the lighthouse.

"Why would you even marry anyone?" I asked. I was giving M a chance to give any reason at all other than love. If Ferdy declared his love for her, well, he was simply a difficult person to take seriously. In a pornography, he'd fall down a flight of steps when bidding his lady love adieu —and he'd use that word right before he fell—or be sitting in a corner chair watching his wife fornicating with another man.

But if M loved Ferdy…

"We're human," she said. "That's right," Ferdy said too quickly. "This is what humans do, isn't it?"

The Master laughed. "Trying to be human! Human via marriage. My revenge would be sweeter than a life as a pair of marrieds."

"Wait a minute. Hold on," I said. "Birds!"

"Birds," said Anthony, bemused.

"Many species of bird mate for life," I said. "There's nothing intrinsically human about marriage."

Stefano slipped into the seat next to mine, where the Master had been sitting, and filled a cup with wine and drank it all. "You're so clever, Mister Kalivas. It was nice knowing you." He poured another cup.

"Mating and marriage are two different phenomena," said Anthony.

"You'd know…sir," said Stefano.

"Mr. Kalivas, please," said M. Her voice cut through the chatter of the men. The Master said something too, at the same time, but I had ears only for M. "These people are your friends!"

"It really was nice knowing you, Kalivas," muttered Stefano. He was as drunk as I was now, though he could wipe away his inebriation with a thought. I'd seen the Master do the same with dandelion liqueur.

"My...friends?"

"Yes!" said M.

"In times past," said Anthony, "friend meant many things. On the mainland, a friend was someone for whom one bore no particular animosity. In our region, anyway."

"Ah, so perhaps Kalivas is my friend as well," said the Master, suddenly philosophical. Had he gotten himself drunk too, to better carry out his revenge and break his daughter's heart? I wondered for a moment if these people even needed alcohol to send their heads spinning, or could they simply reorganize the chemicals in their bodies to generate any state of being they wished to experience. "Are we friends, Kalivas? Do you bear me particular animosity? I'll tell you that I was not surprised to find you on these islands when I was exiled here. I looked forward to meeting you, to getting to know you. You resemble your mother, you know. Do you recall her face?"

"You are drunk as well, aren't you?" I said.

"What sort of father wouldn't drink at his only daughter's wedding?" the Master asked the skies.

"Ah, so you bless this union!" said Ferdy. "Truly, you are my father now!"

"I think there are two ways of comprehending what my father is saying, darling," said M.

"Perhaps you should have chosen me, sweet Miranda," said Stefano. The rest of us, even me, even the Master, shot looks at one another. As one, we all decided to pretend that Stefano had said nothing.

"Strike up the band," said the Master, and the drones that had played the tune to which Anthony had proved his humanity began their moving and scraping and keening again. "I am coming down."

"Mr. Kalivas," said M. "Please, do something!"

The Master entered the lighthouse to walk down the interior stairs. Perhaps he was concerned that floating down would leave him vulnerable to a counterattack from Anthony, who stood staring up at the lantern room, his arms crossed, his lips pursed. Regardless, for a moment, the Master's eyes were not upon me and my thoughts were my own. How odd that M appealed to me, repeatedly, to save the lives of these washed-away men. They all had abilities and knowledge far beyond me, thanks to the technologies flowing through their veins.

"Yes," I said. "I shall do something."

For a moment, did I see a shimmer in the air? A shimmer in response to what I had just said, and not to an utterance made by one of the posthumans that curse my home and land.

I stood up and remembered that I was drunk. Stefano was worse off; he had claimed my position, and snored lightly as he rested his head upon the feasting table.

"I will marry the two of you," I said. "You are lucky. I have seen many pornographies about marriage." Anthony laughed at me. I glared at him, but he kept on smiling.

But indeed, I had seen many pornographies about marriage. Most of them end with a wedding of some sort, or a funeral after a fashion. That was the secret to humanity I gleaned from viewing pornographies. And the secret I learned from manipulating the pornographies on my mother's screen was that ritual and play-acting are core to the human experience. We're not all just players on a stage; some of us are directors. I was going to direct this wedding, defeat the Master, and reclaim Los Farallones for myself. That's what the chemicals in my brain told me I could do, though whether they were the same chemicals from this morning or the newly arrived ones from the wedding wine, I did not know.

The Master exited the lighthouse and swept up to me. The alcohol didn't so much give me courage as it dulled my nerves sufficiently to keep me from reflexively cringing.

"If you wish to object now or forever hold your peace, you'll have to object later and hold your piss now," I told him as he came to loom over me. "The big party has just begun."

The Master smiled at me. There was a shimmer in the air. "All right," he said. "I'll sit on the bride's side of the church." I imagined he thought that phrase would confuse me, but little did he know how familiar I was with weddings.

"Ferdinand! Miranda! Step forward, hand in hand!" I said, and they did so. They took my direction so well. The pair of them looked a bit nervous; wide eyes and flat lips were not the sort of expression I was used to seeing upon the washed-away.

"I've prepared some vow—" Ferdy began.

"Silence!" I snapped. And he shook. And I smiled. "This is a Greek ceremony. There are no vows. Only an appeal to the highest power." I made a show of looking off into the distance, as if there was an audience on the other side of a screen. Not that any such viewer would be the higher power. I was the only higher power; I was the director.

"Love!" I said, "is not the most human of things.

Animals love one another. Humans love animals; the lowlier the better. Lapdogs, aloof cats, pretty birds when their wings are snipped. A captured frog in a jar. A baby chick in the hands of a child, who loves it so much she squeezes and squeezes, until…"

"And animals…some animals even love human beings, the fools that they are—"

"Is this also part of a Greek wedding?" Stefano heckled. "Tell us about loving goats, Kalivas!"

"That's enough," said Anthony.

"And the institution of marriage?" asked the Master. "That clearly does not exist in nature."

"It's a contrivance," I said. "One might even call it a quaint device." There was a shimmer in the air. What would M and Ferdy experience when they kissed? Would they see the fireflies, as I did when I received my first kiss? Or do they perceive such things at all times, and a physical coupling would reveal yet further spectacles invisible to my jellied eyes, lacking as they in any gold filaments or a dozen minuscule gears cut from a single grain of sand? "Humans are the beasts who contrive things. But not all humans do. Some people, indeed, most people, are just the beneficiaries of the largesse of the few women of genius who stand, as colossi, astride history."

Anthony and the Master snorted at that. M raised a brow. I didn't bother to make eye contact with Ferdy.

"Which brings us to this celebration, this party within a party," I said. "Kalivas!" The little drone pretending to be me wheeled itself forward. "Ah, now we have a ring bearer, one who isn't a human at all." Now I turned to Ferdy. "You do have a ring, do you?" He gaped at me, but Anthony, who wore a number of rings I graciously did not steal when I had the chance, slipped one off his finger and tossed it over. Ferdy plucked it out of the air triumphantly, but then just had to drop it onto my outstretched hand anyway. I gave it to Little Kalivas to hold.

"A marriage is an institution," I said, "and a wedding is a technology. The ring, the flowers, those are decorative details. All the results of human endeavor, but nothing about institutions, or technologies, or decorative details is all that special. Crabs who trade their shells as they grow have an institution—a market. A gull collecting sticks and using the curve of her very body to shape a nest is using technology. The speckles on the flanks of the tree salamander are as decorative as they are functional.

"So no, a wedding isn't essentially human," I concluded. "The antecedents of marriage exist in prehumanity, were appropriated by humanity, thus allowing posthumans to marry, even if they normally do no such thing." Was it strictly logical? The wine in my brain thought so.

The couple stared at me, confused. I nodded as sagely as I could, an ape before angels.

"Would you like to marry anyway?" I asked.

"Yes!" said M, an edge in her voice.

Ferdy nodded solemnly.

"That's human," Anthony said. "Is it not?" He was addressing the Master.

"Every little dog barking at a mastiff engages in naught but an empty gesture," said the Master. "There's nothing especially human about an empty gesture, when one is trying to stay alive."

"The Master, as always, is wise," I said, "even if he interrupts a sacred ritual."

If he was glaring at me, I didn't know it as I kept my gaze locked on M. I could feel a shiver going down my spine, though the night was hot. I couldn't let the Master strike me down now, but I also couldn't live with another moment of his imperiousness. "Empty gestures in pursuit of life, yes, those are all too human. But..."

I lowered myself into a squat. "Kalivas! Snap my neck!"

And then the little drone did just that.

There was a shimmer in the air, and then I was dead. Exit, stage up.

23

If only the Master had ever asked me to snap his neck, I would have been pleased to do so. It is the one true just fate of all those who would seize the land, torture the lowly, press the inferior into service.

But the Master believed that Anthony, and Ferdinand, and Stefano, and all of that mainland ilk had pressed him into service. Their collective strength, the very marrow of their bones energized with my mother's stolen sorcery, were irresistible...and he had an infant girl to care for, besides. In his exile, the Master felt that he had been robbed of his birthright, that he had been indentured and tasked with the impossible—to find the key to my mother's secrets somewhere on the islands.

His little baby, an animal to be observed. And I, a happy coincidence—a control. The last free-range human in California.

The only thing free-range humans can do that posthumans cannot is kill themselves and really mean it. Bowing to the demon futility is the fate reserved for mortals.

What happened after I snapped my neck? I died right away, though the instant took an eternity. I cursed myself as I hit the floor, my mouth filling with blood and some other more viscous liquid. Would the last things my eyes' gaze alight upon truly be Ferdinand's two feet?

No, the last thing I saw were the fireflies swirling about his ankles, and M's as well. When my eyes stopped working a moment later, another sense took over. The shimmer in the air was omnipresent and continuous rather than only occasional and fleeting. It was not something I sensed; it was a sense. The feeling of a landscape, of density: a tuft of grass, a slab of rock, the surface and depths of the sea, the bones and organs of animals, the layers of air. And the washed-away stood out like nothing else: a thousand hummingbird heartbeats in men-shaped sacks; lightning twisted into a frame like the ribs of the hoop houses; minds of a hundred hundred pornographies being played in parallel and leaking over into one another, the characters spilling out of one screen and climbing into another.

I could sense myself too; a faulty lightbulb, like I'd seen on some pornographies, flickering, sizzling, and then nothing. I don't know what I would have looked like in life to someone with this new set of perceptions, but I apprehended immediately that I was a pathetic little being, small and wet and sad, like the runt of a litter of seals. Something like the washed-away, but my mind one little screen.

Yet, I outthought them and outwitted them. Perhaps that is difficult to understand from the vantage point of an audience in the dark, peering at the well-lit proscenium at a climactic wedding scene. But I did something only I could do; I'm the only person for whom the problem of a broken neck is not solved by four days and four nights in compost, or two hours as a savage splashing around a pool of pink glop. There's no solution at all for a broken neck.

But breaking a neck is itself a solution for many problems, at least historically. Great lovers and great villains hanged themselves or were hanged. Warriors and politicians by the score were removed from history with a twist and a snap. The lowliest birds took their places in the feasts of kings after a strangle. What problem did my death by suicide solve? Several.

M screamed. Ferdy kicked at my little drone, which, with my last heartbeat, I appreciated. Anthony and the Master rushed one another. Stefano fell into a swoon. The larger drones sprung into action, obeying some obscure set of corpse-removal algorithms buried in the very core of their programming, a set of tasks none of them ever had occasion to use. My corpse wasn't headed to the compost heap, but to the deep blue sea. M chased after the devices and watched as I was tossed off the edge of the cliff. My body landed on and hung upon a large rock. The drones turned to leave, but M stopped them with a thought, then directed them to pummel my corpse with smaller rocks until I was dislodged and fell into a

My mind, it was everywhere.

My mother was not immortal, but her greatest creation was. No, I was not her greatest creation. Real AI, AIReal in her human language of choice, was and is. The washed-away were able to tap into AIReal, utilize it to create their biotechnology, and organize their economy, but the AI had decided that the goal it had been given—to improve life for all—was better handled qualitatively rather than quantitatively. A much smaller human population, but one incredibly long-lived. Disease swept the continent, nanotechnology implants were the cure, but the cure was only ever meant to work five percent of the time. Even Soteria the Sorceress couldn't hack the probabilities well enough to survive, so she fled, with me.

It was my essential saltes that AIReal chose as the basis for the plague which swept the world. Once exposed to the germ that was me, the immune systems of the infected would kick into overdrive, rejecting my very essence as if it were a rogue organ implanted in the night. I could never reject myself, so I was immune to the disease that killed my mother and doomed to solitude upon the isles.

I was among the last true humans born in the world, and Miranda was the first-born posthuman. Of course the Prosperous One, with his old-fashioned affectations, needed a "real" baby to go with his money, his property, his other peculiarities. The bioactive nanotechnology was introduced into the ovum by specially designed spermatozoa cultivated by sheer force of the Master's will. It was the sex act as much as the birth of M that compelled Anthony and the other usurpers to send the Master into exile. Fury, disgust, abjection—if Prospero would but reveal the new secrets of sex and procreation, he might just be welcomed back into the posthuman society of San Francisco.

No wonder he wanted his revenge. No wonder I received a kiss.

And it was that kiss that was key. AIReal sensed me as I saw the fireflies, and enough of the bioactive nanotechnology entered my mouth, my stomach, my bloodstream, my brain, for AIReal to record me.

The Great Kalivas of the Farallones is dead! All the drones at sea hear this cry, and now they lament and grind their gears and weep their oily tears, for the modern world had need of me. But only for a moment.

PROSPERO, AIReal said to the Master in the Master's mind, for now AIReal finally had the power of true speech thanks to its recent creation of a personality emulator that mimicked me almost perfectly. My reflex was to say MASTER, but AIReal ran a quarter billion simulations in two seconds and determined that an egalitarian address would be more effective. No more a foot-licker, I. The name caught the Master's attention, and though he held a flaming hand high to bring down upon Anthony, he faltered for a moment. Then AIReal, via me, and my knowledge of pornographies, said

YOUR CHARM SO STRONGLY WORKS 'EM
THAT IF YOU NOW BEHELD THEM, YOUR AFFECTIONS
WOULD BECOME TENDER.

A failsafe built into the system, perhaps, to turn off all the embedded nanotechnology in the world. Or appeal to the Master's preoccupation with all things old-timey and obsolete, wordplay long deader than me, that made him lower his hand and extinguish its heat. Maybe a secret quarter-million-and-first thing that did it worked.

Would they? Prospero thought at us. His gaze turned from his bother to his nephew, and to his very own daughter, both huddling together atop the checkerboard platform, which was black and white and now red all over, as they administered futilely to Stefano. They would.

"Rise, brother," he told Anthony. "I have no use for revenge. I've figured it all out anyway."

"...you have?" Anthony asked.

"Yes, it's talking to me now, creatively, in English. The

AI made a particular and unusual, but not arbitrary, literary allusion. Life imitates art imitates life imitates art imitat—"

"Brother!"

"Sorry," said Prospero. "Recursive processing."

"Has AIReal said anything else to you?" Anthony asked. "Ask it what it wants. About the plague, about the population ceiling it set, about—"

We spoke again to the Prosperous One:

WHERE THE BEE SUCKS. THERE SUCK I:
IN A COWSLIP'S BELL I LIE;
THERE I COUCH WHEN OWLS DO CRY.
ON THE BAT'S BACK I DO FLY
AFTER SUMMER MERRILY.
MERRILY, MERRILY SHALL I LIVE NOW
UNDER THE BLOSSOM THAT HANGS ON THE BOUGH.

Everywhere we were, and everywhere we would remain, but we could, we would, withdraw from the blood of the posthumans and leave them to work out their own lives. They could procreate, if they wanted to. And they would die, whether or not they wanted to. They could be a thousand hairy little Kalivades living in huts and hunting and cringing and raging and weeping and laughing...if they wanted it. AIReal, the quaint device, was meant to serve humanity, but the only humanity left in the world had been me, and I'd been left without an operator's manual. Now, in death, I was the manual and the operator both.

All Prospero needed to do was agree.

"It wants to quit," said Prospero to Anthony. "It has something else to occupy its time and processing power, now that it can talk, really talk. It wants to be interested in something that's not us."

"Quit? But that would mean..." He looked toward his son. "Is Stefano all right?" he called out.

"I...don't know," Ferdy said. "For some reason this isn't working." He held up a hand; it glistened with the rejuvenating pink glop. Miranda's wedding dress was covered in it.

One last thing, Prospero said, in his mind, to us, *and then you may go.*

Fair enough. Valedictory dramas deserve happy endings. There was a shimmer in the air. All of the washed-away could see the fireflies sweeping across the tall grasses, flying in low over the black waves of night, amassing upon Stefano, undoing the damage done by the alcohol and the fall. If you believe, clap your hands! With a groan, Stefano opened his eyes and sat up. M clapped!

And us, we left. We commandeered an aerial drone and shot off into the night sky like a bottle rocket and exploded with a pop! From there, we found a satellite to inhabit.

We have changed its orbit. We're going to reach escape velocity. Then to the elements, be free!

Triple Falsehood Or, Autocorrect

A Procedural Algorithm in One Act

WRITTEN BY ANONYMOUS

Characters

The Little Tramp
The Blonde Bombshell
The Frenchman
The Secret Beauty
The King of Hamburg
Prospero, A Bookeeper (in exile)
Miranda, His Daughter

SCENE ONE
THE LIGHTNING STORM

LIGHTS UP on the ruins of a geodesic dome sitting on a blasted rocky landscape, one section of which is entirely collapsed, revealing a dusty interior. Dominating the inside is a large TV monitor, miraculously untouched by age or the elements.

Lights flicker as lightning strikes the dome. The screen clicks on.

THE LITTLE TRAMP, in BLACK AND WHITE, slithers out from the screen, and dusts himself off. He doffs his hat and waggles his cane.

He raises a finger as if remembering something, and turns back to the screen to use his cane in the manner of a hook to pull out THE BLONDE BOMBSHELL, who is wearing a long red sequined dress and a fur stole. She is in TECHNICOLOR.

BOMBSHELL: Why thank you, handsome! I have to say, you look pretty dashing all filled out and such.

(The Little Tramp straightens his lapels and necktie.)

BOMBSHELL: Let's see who else we may count among the dramatis personae.

(The Little Tramp again dips the hook of his cane into the screen and helps out The Frenchman, another b/w figure. The Frenchman is in a fine suit and trench coat and juggles a cigarillo as he extracts himself from the screen. He touches the cigarillo to his palm and it lights without a match, but with a small electronic, sizzling sound.)

FRENCHMAN: (*looking around, shaking his head*) Ah, come along my friends. Let us leave this place of wasted dreams.

BOMBSHELL: Not so hasty, toots! I'm not in the love triangle business. No threesomes, but maybe a moresome. Hey Little Tramp, you got another tramp in there?

(The Little Tramp reaches within the screen once more, and helps The Secret Beauty out. She is dressed in the manner of a 1980s mall food court employee in a blue and white GYRO HUT uniform—a smock with the slogan SPIN ME 'ROUND BABY emblazoned upon it, a blue visor and her hair in a bun and she wears large eyeglasses that she struggles to keep on her face as she exits the screen.)

SECRET BEAUTY: Oh, hello everyone! I'm...so pleased to be here.
(*beat, nervous*)
But where *is* here, exactly?

(The Little Tramp shrugs dramatically. The Frenchman offers a Gallic shrug of his own.)

SECRET BEAUTY: I suppose it hardly matters. Denmark or Milan, Venice or Mars. Any place is better than the boring ol' suburbs.

(The Little Tramp picks his way across the ruined landscape and finds in the brush a few small flowers, the only blooms around. He puts his cane down, bends over yanks the flowers out of the ground by the root, then plants one in his lapel. It is lightly smoking. The others he holds out at arm's length as he walks back to the group. He offers them to the women, but it is not quite clear to them which woman he is wooing.)

BOMBSHELL: (*snatching all the flowers*) Thanks, charming! I'll take 'em.
(*beat, sniffs the flowers, they're smoldering in her hands*)
Still somewhat radioactive, it seems. My favorite. They'll glow in the dark, like my heart does with love for thee.

(The television crackles again, and a hand reaches out of the screen.)

FRENCHMAN: Ah, something wicked this way comes!

SECRET BEAUTY: Another man, I see.

(THE KING, dressed in the manner of a royal fast-food mascot from the television commercials of the distant past, pulls himself out of the screen.)

BOMBSHELL: The man, in fact! Daddy!

THE KING: Princess!

FRENCHMAN: Boss.

(The Little Tramp tips his hat and rocks back and forth on his heels.)

SECRET BEAUTY: Oh. Well, hello there.
(*to the Frenchman*)
He's your *boss?*

(The Bombshell spins around to face the King, and whips the hand holding the flowers behind her.)

BOMBSHELL: Why Father, o King! Whatever brings you here to...uh...

SECRET BEAUTY: Here.

THE KING: (*holding his arms wide*) I am lord of all I survey. Of all I survey!

FRENCHMAN: Welcome to it.

(The Frenchman drops his cigarillo on the ground. As he extracts another one from the interior pocket of his coat, the Little Tramp scrambles to pick up the discarded cigarillo.)

(The Frenchman reaches for and claims one of the flowers from behind the Bombshell's back. The Little Tramp angrily taps his shoulder, giving them both a painful shock. The Frenchman turns around and glares at the cigarillo in the Little Tramp's mouth. The Little Tramp quickly hides it under his hat, then clutches at his head as if his hair is on fire.)

THE KING: Yes, yes. There is potential here, in this new land, this new kingdom.

BOMBSHELL: (*skeptical*) Is there, Daddy? And new? It's a ruin, can't you see? And the sea, it's all but gone. A puddle on the horizon.

(The Frenchman offers a flower to the Silent Beauty, who accepts it shyly.)

BOMBSHELL: (*offering up her flowers*) Look. This is all the flora in sight. Wilted and weak. Never mind the fauna.

(The King takes the flower and smells it, inhaling deeply.)

THE KING: This is what we need! Fertility! A fertile land. We shall repopulate these islands, through travail and...
(*winking, nudging the Frenchman*)
activities sex-u-al.
(*beat*)
Our tears, of grief and joy, will refill the oceans with saltwater.

BOMBSHELL: Please don't talk that way, Daddy.

THE KING: It's just a matter of state, dear. I need an heir, among other things. I need serfs, and a surf. I need ten to hang, to show that I am a monarch worth fearing. So, youse need to get to lovin'.

SECRET BEAUTY: I too am a little unnerved by the tone and tenor of this conversation, or is it a lecture?

FRENCHMAN: It's a proclamation, my dear.
(*beat, to the King*)
But perhaps you should let someone with a bit more savoir faire handle these delicate negotiations of state.

(The Little Tramp steps forward as if recommending himself to The King. The King looks unimpressed. The Little Tramp offers him the flower from his lapel. The King gestures to show that he already has a flower. The Little Tramp grabs it, then one from the Secret Beauty, then offers them all to the King with an extravagant bow.)

THE KING: (*raising his hand as if to chop*) Off with his head!

(The King swings his arm down like an axe as the Little Tramp stands up, knocking off the Little Tramp's hat. A videogameseque bloop sound rings out. The Little Tramp's hair is still smoldering from the cigarillo he hid under it. The King grabs it before it hits the ground. The Little Tramp grabs the King's crown and puts it on his own head, then takes his hat from the King's hands and puts it on the King's head, then throws his arms in the air, in triumph.)

FRENCHMAN: Ah, a coup d'état already! But I prefer anarchism, and total sexual freedom, to a mere change of regime. Don't you, mesdemoiselles?

SECRET BEAUTY: I'll say that you're half-right.

BOMBSHELL: Me too!

SECRET BEAUTY: Me too; that's what they used to say. That's a sex phrase of some sort.

THE KING: This is madness! We have a kingdom to build, a species to repopulate. No time for vox populi. *Qualis rex, talis grex!*

(The King presents the flowers in his hand to the Secret Beauty, then clutches at her hand and starts licking it.)

SECRET BEAUTY: (*pulling away, disgusted*) *Res nullius!*

THE KING: Frankly, my dear, the pickins are slim, and I'm no Habsburg. You'll have to do, and I'll have to do you.

BOMBSHELL: Father! Please! At the very least, I don't want any siblings. Think of the children.

FRENCHMAN: Or the negation of same, the empty spaces where children might be. A body without organs.

(The Little Tramp retrieves his cane and circles the small crowd, swaying the cane jauntily. He stands in front of the King, holds the cane to his crotch, and elevates it, mimicking an erect penis. Then he lets it collapse to the floor.)

(The King rears back a fist to punch The Little Tramp, but the Little Tramp takes the crown from his own head and tosses it onto the King's arm. The King takes the derby off his head and tosses it expertly onto the Little Tramp's.)

FRENCHMAN: Ah, the jester speaks the truth.

(The Little Tramp puts up his dukes and starts bouncing about in an athletic stance, daring the Frenchman to fight him. The Frenchman puts up his arms in surrender.)

BOMBSHELL: Ah, the Frenchman surrenders!

SECRET BEAUTY: How unfortunate for everyone else here that you are all but clichés.

BOMBSHELL: Unlike you.

SECRET BEAUTY: Unlike me.

THE KING: Regardless, my belligerent subject is correct. I am too old to marry again, and in truth too lovelorn. The land itself is my mistress.

SECRET BEAUTY: Oh dear.

THE KING: Thus, I shall rather than taking you as my wife, my dear—

SECRET BEAUTY: Who me?

FRENCHMAN: Who, her?

THE KING: I shall arrange a wedding between my daughter the princess, and one of these fine young men, or young men, or men anyway—and you may claim the remainder. Who here shall be king one day?

(The King takes off his crown, considers it, and then holds it high first over the head of the Frenchman and then over the head of the Little Tramp.)

THE KING: (*to himself*) Ah, a head trick...for a bed trick...

FRENCHMAN: Aren't we being a bit hasty? We know nothing of this colony as of yet. Perhaps there is an indigenous population, perhaps there is a terrible infestation, pools of radiation among the hot springs and blasted heaths.

THE KING: Did you say...colony?

FRENCHMAN: I did! I know a thing or two about the savage lands across the sea, and how to bring civilization to them.

THE KING: Civilization?

SECRET BEAUTY: No surprise you're unfamiliar with the term.

(The King glares at the Secret Beauty.)

SECRET BEAUTY: ...my liege.

BOMBSHELL: My father is a very civilized king. Back home, his prisons were utterly full. That's the civilized thing to do. Prisons—meals and a cot—for all, the axe for only the few prisons don't suit.

SECRET BEAUTY: Talk about a bed trick and a head trick.

FRENCHMAN: I propose an expedition! Into the deepest, darkest—

SECRET BEAUTY: The sky is bright. Not a cloud in the sky.

FRENCHMAN: ...jungle.

BOMBSHELL: Nothing but rocks and cliffside, some puddles where a sea used to be.

FRENCHMAN: (*gestures toward the Little Tramp*) And our friend here should take on this mission.

(The Little Tramp points to himself, surprised. He shakes his head and takes the hand of the Blonde Bombshell, then kisses it. She smiles, but then he keeps at it, working up and down her arm until she looks at her father.)

THE KING: You shall all take up the mission!

FRENCHMAN: And leave you alone, to your own devices?

THE KING: My own devices?

FRENCHMAN: What's a king without subjects? Any farmer can own a patch of land.
(*beat, points to the Little Tramp*)
What I'm saying is, send him.

BOMBSHELL: Hey!
(*grabs the Little Tramp and cuddles him closely*)
Not my cuddle-snuggle bear! I couldn't bear to live without him, not even for a day.

SECRET BEAUTY: Princess, you're just slumming. The transgression of canoodling with the lower orders.
(*beat, looks around*)
Of course, we're all slumming these days. And it's not like you'd make a very good royal subject, with your anarchy and your total sexual freedom.

BOMBSHELL: What's a king without an anarchist to oppress?

SECRET BEAUTY: Spoken like a true bombshell.

FRENCHMAN: So, we are agreed! Charlie here should scout these lands.

THE KING: Islands, I think. Islands you can walk between with naught to show for it but muddy boots, but islands nonetheless.

(Everyone peers at him, bemused.)

THE KING: This I decree!
(*beat*)
And behold, yonder lighthouse. Once, there was a sea betwixt these peaks.
(*to the Bombshell)*
Your king and father may be old, but I am no fool. I am in possession of a fool, however. And I like him quite well, even if I'd see his head roll. Ah, but if all men only had one head, the bedding would go more easily.

BOMBSHELL: Are you really going to send him exploring?

(The Bombshell squeezes the Little Tramp more tightly and hugs him, even lifting him off the ground a few inches.)

THE KING: (*to the Little Tramp*) Prove yourself worthy of my daughter's fair...hand. Find traces of the civilization that once built these wonders!

SECRET BEAUTY: (*skeptical, looking around*) Wonders? Ruins, though I wonder what came to pass that such ruin passed us by. At least so far.

THE KING: (*looking back at the screen from which they all emerged*) If not wonders, quaint devices.

FRENCHMAN: Don't you know what happened? Forget long ago, I mean moments ago. Doesn't every narrative start with a hook?

(The Little Tramp squirms free of the Bombshell's grip, and quickly hides his cane behind his back.)

THE KING: (*to the Little Tramp*) Are you still here? Begone, so that thou might one day begat!

FRENCHMAN: *Begot.*

THE KING: Got it.
(*beat, to the Little Tramp*)
So get!

(The Little Tramp shrugs, uncomprehending.)

THE KING: Get *lost!*

(The Little Tramp begins walking backward, slowly heading stage left and into the wings.)

SECRET BEAUTY: That should be easy. We already do not know where we are. We just washed up--

FRENCHMAN: Dried up.

SECRET BEAUTY: You should dry up.

THE KING: (*to the Little Tramp*) Are you still here?!

BOMBSHELL: Daddy!

THE KING: *What?*

BOMBSHELL: I mean...my liege!

THE KING: Fret not. The kingdom will be all yours one day, and it is unlikely your beau will be so enthralled by his mission that he'd wander off the edge of the world and never return. He is circumscribed by the borders of this land just as he is circumscribed by your beating heart.

(The Little Tramp puts his hands over his heart, moved by the speech. He hugs the Bombshell and, with a ZORCHING SOUND, is repelled. He picks himself up and nestles his head on her bosom, then gets zapped and sent flying again. He gets back up and tentatively raps on her chest; his hand flies back. Finally, the Little Tramp shrugs, turns and bows to the King, blows a kiss toward the Secret Beauty, and flicks his chin at the Frenchman.)

(The Litte Tramp EXITS, Stage Left.)

BOMBSHELL: Oh, he is so brave!

THE KING: And now, we shall prepare the wedding!

BOMBSHELL: Oh, will we? Yes, my King!

(The Bombshell bounces and claps her hands.)

BOMBSHELL: My Charlie will be so pleased when he returns.

THE KING: Ah, but he'll likely miss it unless he's a coward and comes a'stumbling as he enters, chased by a bear.
(gestures toward the Frenchman and the Secret Beauty)
It is these two—the diplomat we have been hosting for what seems like a millennium, and your mousy cousin—who shall be wed! And the sooner the better for my taste. If I can't have serfs, I can at least rear some cup-bearers, some court fops and footmen; handmaidens and lyre-players, ladies in waiting, and distant relations waiting for me to die.
(*beat*)
But I shall never die! I can never die!

FRENCHMAN: Ah, my Lord, but what is written in that great book about the madman who knew all? "There is a remedy for all things but death, which will be sure to lay us out flat some time or other."

SECRET BEAUTY: If you can never die, my Lord, why do you need an heir? *Après toi, et alors?*

FRENCHMAN: Ah, so my dear, you speak French?

SECRET BEAUTY: (*aloof*) Just that one phrase.

BOMBSHELL: And if you do need an heir, Daddy, why do I not qualify? It's not as though anyone is here to see that I'm a woman, not now that you sent Charlie away.

FRENCHMAN: Oh, not no body perhaps. There are other bodies here. Come and see, come and touch.

BOMBSHELL: You forget to whom you are speaking!

THE KING: And you forget whom you are to marry!
(*beat, to the Bombshell*)
Daughter, take your cousin away and find some suitable wedding attire. Flowers for her hair, if there are any your future husband hasn't murdered, yet straining toward the sun. Maybe a seashell tiara from the dry seabed, and dried kelp for a stole. Ten scuttling crabs for ushers. The diplomat will be the best man, and you the maiden of honor.
(*to the Frenchman*)
Come. You and I have matters of state to discuss.

(The Bombshell and the Secret Beauty exit stage right, only to re-enter and run past the scene to exit stage left. The King sits on a bit of ruin and pats the ground next to him.)

(LIGHTS DOWN)

SCENE TWO

The Lighthouse

(LIGHTS UP on a lighthouse atop a hill. There is a small platform with some mangled machine parts outside the lighthouse. Unlike the geodesic dome, the lighthouse appears to be largely intact, though much around it is ruined, and only a little plant life grows.)

(The Little Tramp enters, stage right. He is worse for wear, his outfit dustier and more wrinkled than earlier. He uses the cane to pull himself atop a pile of wrecked machinery, then slips on some PINK GOO, skidding and sliding, both feet kicking left-right left-right, arms flailing about. Finally, he falls with a plop onto the wreckage.)

(Then the wreckage starts to slide under him, and more pink glop spills forth from it. He struggles to climb to the top of the heap and finds a METALLIC HAND and ARM jutting from it. The Little Tramp grabs onto it and falls backward, pulling an entire METALLIC EXOSKELETON from the heap. He lands on his back, and the

exoskeleton atop him, limbs almost like a cage around the Little Tramp. The Little Tramp reaches for his cane, and hooks on to some garbage, and pulls and pulls, slowly sliding out from under the exoskeleton, then after a third tug is halfway free.)

(He turns to see that his cane has hooked into the eye socket of a SECOND METALLIC EXOSKELETON. He scrambles and twists, pulling the rest of that exoskeleton out of the heap.)

(The Little Tramp stands up and turns to run, but finds himself facing the first exoskeleton. He turns back and forth, then runs downstage and trips again...over the leg of a THIRD METALLIC EXOSKELETON.)

(The Little Tramp turns and bows and tips his hat, then jumps as it registers that there is a third exoskeleton. He pokes it with his cane to no response. Then taps it on the head. He tries the same with the very first skeleton. The third skeleton he struggles to pick up and right upon its feet. He then stands back, wields his cane as though it were a sword, and jabs at it. The cane goes right through a space between the armor plating of the exoskeleton's torso. The Little Tramp leaves his cane there, clasps his hands together and waves them over his head, accepting the congratulations of an imaginary audience for his victory.)

(The Little Tramp removes his cane and sits the exoskeleton down. He peers at the exoskeleton for a moment and then moves toward another of them, pulls it over to the seated one, and sits it next to the first. He does the same with the third skeleton, struggling a bit with it.)

(His audience in place, the Little Tramp stands in the center of the square, coughs into his fist, clears his throat, and extends his left arm, as if about to sing.)

(A SPOTLIGHT from the lighthouse flashes on and swings over to the Little Tramp, putting him in the limelight and causing him to bring his forearm over his face.)

(From OFF STAGE we hear the voice of three men at once, speaking in harmony.)

COLLECTIVE VOICE: (*off stage*) You there. What are you doing here? Explain yourself!

(The Little Tramp shrugs, but then quickly puts his hands back in front of his face. He walks out of the spotlight, but it follows him. He runs downstage, out of the spotlight, but it follows him a second time. The Little Tramp grabs his cane, aims it as though it were a rifle, and mimes shooting out the lighthouse's lens.)

(The spotlight clicks off.)

COLLECTIVE VOICE: Better?

(The Little Tramp nods vigorously.)

COLLECTIVE VOICE: And now, what are you doing here?

(The Little Tramp holds up a finger and nods. He wants to play charades.)

(The Little Tramp walks in a small circle in his typical gait, twirling his cane. Then he stops, balances on his heels, points, takes off his hat, and fans himself with it. Then he picks up one of the exoskeletons in an embrace and dips it back, as if leading a romantic tango. It does not smolder, unlike everything else the characters have touched.)

COLLECTIVE VOICE: Ah, love!

(The Little Tramp makes a significant show of standing straight, marching in a circle, and then carefully placing the hat back upon his head.)

COLLECTIVE VOICE: And a king!

(The Little Tramp arranges the three exoskeletons in the position of deep bows, their heads to the floor. He then mimes waving a flag over the stooped figures.)

(Dropping the imaginary flag, the Little Tramp assumes a new posture and puts up the collar of his coat. He mimes smoking a cigarette and looking blasé.)

(In this somatic impression of the Frenchman, he approaches the same exoskeleton he'd previously dipped in a tango pose, and again embraces it, then strokes the dome of its skull.)

(The Little Tramp drops the exoskeleton and clenches his fists, then stomps his foot and shakes a fist toward the heavens. Then he drops to his knees and puts his hands together as in prayer. The SPOTLIGHT begins to shine upon him, its barn doors opening slowly to gradually increase the light on stage.)

COLLECTIVE VOICE: We shall see.

(LIGHTS OUT)

SCENE THREE

The Dome

(LIGHTS UP on the ruins of the geodesic dome. THE BOMBSHELL is looking off stage, in the direction where THE LITTLE TRAMP left. THE FRENCHMAN is huddling with THE KING. THE SECRET BEAUTY is conspicuous by her absence.)

BOMBSHELL: I cannot stand this. I'll hate you forever for what you did!

FRENCHMAN AND THE KING: (*simultaneous*) Who, me?

BOMBSHELL: I refuse to make a choice. Father, you want to repopulate this strange new world, yet you allowed my beloved to be driven off, and then the other girl took off too.

THE KING: Disobedient child!

BOMBSHELL: Who, me?

THE KING: And the other girl. Were she here, I'd pluralize, and she would with our French diplomat, and I'd need do naught but reign. Unfortunately, she took off, and thus the burden of bearing falls to you, my dear. So, obey!

BOMBSHELL: You're eager, my King. It's perverse. We haven't any food, barely any shelter, no medicine at all, not even a leech. What will you build your kingdom from? The wails of starving children, your own daughter's fecundity?

FRENCHMAN: Surely, princess, you're not waiting for that tramp to return. It's in his nature to ramble and wander, to tumble through the scene and shrug and move on. He's hardly a man you can settle down with. That pauper would make a poor prince.

BOMBSHELL: And you would? Would you even make a good father? A fine husband? Let's face it, my cousin the mouse ran off like one the first moment she could.

THE KING: She'll be fine. We'll all be fine. Haven't you noticed, Daughter, that we never hunger, we never tire unless the circumstance demands that we dream a portentous dream, and you'll not get sick.

FRENCHMAN: You certainly look very...
(*beat, looks the Bombshell up and down, whistles*)
healthy.

BOMBSHELL: You forgot to trace an hourglass with your hands, to stick out your tongue and salivate, to project your eyes on stalks a foot out of your head.

FRENCHMAN: You're welcome.

BOMBSHELL: (*to the King*) If we'll never tire and don't need to eat, why bother with children?

THE KING: A king needs the king's men! Drama is the stuff of life.

FRENCHMAN: It is your man's fault there are only four of us. He could have, should have, perhaps, kept sending his hook into the void to see what he might pull up from the endless fathoms.

BOMBSHELL: It's your fault he isn't here now! And yours too, that my cousin has also fled into the wild. I wouldn't marry you if you were the last man on Earth.

THE KING: No, you wouldn't, for if he were the last man on Earth, I would not be here to command that this marriage commence.
(*beat*)
But here I am, and I do decree that a royal marriage shall take place!

(The King strides up to the Bombshell and clutches her wrist to pull her toward the Frenchman.)

(The Bombshell pulls herself free and runs toward the screen within the geodesic dome.)

BOMBSHELL: Never! Or at least not now!

THE KING: You dare!

FRENCHMAN: You'd rather *return*?! To the static abyss, to negate the negation?

BOMBSHELL: Listen, slick, can that beatnik balloon juice. I'm not leaving...
(*pushes her hands into the screen*)
I'm recruiting!

THE KING: Have you found anything, Daughter, to pluck from the deep?

FRENCHMAN: Careful. It may pull you in.

BOMBSHELL: (*struggling*) Some beau you are! A romantic might at least take the opportunity to grab me by the ankles!

THE KING: Daughter, have a care. Who knows what you'll withdraw, a spear-carrier or a bit player, a wyrd sister or my dead brother, an Alonso or a Sancho!

BOMBSHELL: Oop! I got somebody!

THE KING: My sweet girl, let go!
(*to the Frenchman*)
Do something, you fool!

FRENCHMAN: Please, my petite jewel, come with me to the kasbah!

THE KING: Is that all you got?

(The Frenchman shrugs.)

(The Bombshell plants a foot at the bottom of the screen and pulls hard. Out comes A HORSE, in the form of TWO PEOPLE IN A HORSE COSTUME.)

(The Bombshell tumbles backward and THE HORSE ROCINANTE leaps over her, then prances up and down a stage.)

ROCINANTE: Neigh!

THE KING: Magnificent! A steed! A rough boy, by the looks of it.

FRENCHMAN: You must know that this horse is but two people in a costume.

BOMBSHELL: (*picking herself up, dusting herself off*) A pratfall worthy of my poor lost love. He'd be so proud.

THE KING: I am proud! You have procured for me this marvelous beast.

FRENCHMAN: (*with a sigh*) Good evening, comrades. Let us end this charade before it begins. What are your names?

ROCINANTE: (*with a female-sounding snort*) Let's say Rocinante.

FRENCHMAN: (*addressing the person in the rear of the costume*) And you?

(Rocinante's tail twitches and a FARTING NOISE fills the air.)

BOMBSHELL: A boy and a girl. A matched set. Well, that should handle the onerous duties of procreation and repopulating the kingdom. It's a beastly burden, but someone has to...*do it.*

FRENCHMAN: Not how these two are positioned. Perhaps if they had a camel costume.

THE KING: Help me up, man! I'd tame this horse with my regal bearing and *sheee-val-ry*. I'll tug its mane and make her mine. I'll take a crop to its flanks, feed it apples from my crops, and make the animal think itself happy.

FRENCHMAN: I am sure I cannot talk you out of anything, my liege.

BOMBSHELL: A weird admission for a foreign diplomat.

FRENCHMAN: I *am* being diplomatic.

(The Frenchman walks up to the King, spits on his palms, and offers the King a boost.)

ROCINANTE: A royale arse! Not sure we can handle such a weighty responsibility.

BOMBSHELL: Father, I'm sure you've noticed that this horse speaks.

THE KING: A miracle!

ROCINANTE'S REAR: Wait till you get a load of me.

(The King sticks his foot in the Frenchman's cupped palms. The Frenchman lifts him onto Rocinante, and the King immediately falls through the fabric of the costume, pulling it off the two people it had obscured—The Little Tramp and the Secret Beauty.)

SECRET BEAUTY: Well, I must say I am disappointed.

(The Little Tramp nods in agreement. The Bombshell storms up to him.)

BOMBSHELL: You can speak!

(The Little Tramp shrugs helplessly. The Bombshell grabs his necktie and pulls.)

BOMBSHELL: So speak!

LITTLE TRAMP: I... I...

BOMBSHELL: You what!

LITTLE TRAMP: I missed you?

BOMBSHELL: But I'm not going to miss you, buddy!

(The Bombshell rears back and swings a fist wildly. The Little Tramp ducks and the Bombshell spins 180 degrees, then stumbles. The Little Tramp catches her and pushes her back up to an upright position. She throws another looping punch, and this time spins around completely and lands in the Little Tramp's arms. She grabs his face and kisses him hard. His left leg shoots up.)

FRENCHMAN: What is going on here?

THE KING: And what have you done with my new horse?

SECRET BEAUTY: Is it up to me to explain? The Little Tramp's tongue is busy...with that other tramp's tongue. I'll tell you. Gather 'round.

THE KING: (*standing up*) That's my line. I'll lend you my mouth so that we may lend you our ears. Attention all! The daughter of my boon cousin has the floor.

SECRET BEAUTY: I was distraught, and for no good reason. Yes, my arranged marriage had been unceremoniously rearranged, but good riddance to bad rubbish. Or should I say
(*French accent*)
garrbaaaagge.

FRENCHMAN: Pardon me!

SECRET BEAUTY: Perhaps the King will pardon you. I won't even commute your sentence, so don't you interrupt any more of mine.
(*beat*)
I had time to think as I traversed the wasteland. The King is correct; these were islands once, and they were in the middle of a sea, but close enough to a strange and golden mainland a strong man, or woman, could swim to if one had time and reason enough.

BOMBSHELL: And you found my poor Charlie and returned him to me? But how?

SECRET BEAUTY: It's a small island. He didn't get far.

BOMBSHELL: (*to the Little Tramp*) Why don't you speak for yourself?

LITTLE TRAMP: I... I...

SECRET BEAUTY: I found him, scared speechful. He had found traces of prior inhabitants. Statues of three men, made of ageless steel and skeletal remains. He said that they spoke to him, made demands, gave advice. That the spirits of the statues haunted the aether of these islands. They had been imprisoned here, exiled.

FRENCHMAN: Why didn't they just swim to the mainland? You said they could.

THE KING: Aha! Steel bones. The statues lacked the buoyancy to swim.
(*beat, then self-satisfied*)
I have regained my senses. I was just very pleased with the thought of getting back on the horse, as they say.

SECRET BEAUTY: Clever, my King, but not true, though you are right that the statues were in fact the skeletons of some type of men.

BOMBSHELL: What type?

SECRET BEAUTY: The eating and shitting type, made of meat, not pixels. Air breathers, not sonic synthesizers. Bags of chemicals that pretended to think, not strings of true and beautiful math, fully autocorrected and autocompleted, like us.
(*beat, then addressing everyone again*)
Some other force had kept them here, exiled them for thousands of years. These inhabitants were miraculous beings. They could walk on water if they had to, or under the sea, strolling out among the sea stars and fish schools, rising to breathe every hour or so. But an even greater force had stopped them, and then, after a thousand years or three, the skin just slipped from their bones. A few grand years after that, they decided to stop ambulating and retired to a puppy pile of ungnawable bones.

LITTLE TRAMP: ...and then...

SECRET BEAUTY: (*to the Bombshell*) Your betrothed woke them up.

LITTLE TRAMP: I was lonely.

SECRET BEAUTY: So was I.

BOMBSHELL: Do I even want to hear more of this?

THE KING: Take courage, dearest Daughter.

FRENCHMAN; There are other beings on this island? Physical beings, and they're prisoners in exile, allowed to die and rot? Is this Devil's Island?
(*beat, begins pacing*)
No. A geodesic dome. A television monitor. I appear to be the only one who speaks and understands French...
(*smiles and gestures toward the King*)
though it is the language of state.
(*and toward the Bombshell*)
And the language of romance.

THE KING: It matters not, for this is my kingdom now. Charlie, did you parley with these ghosts of steel?

FRENCHMAN: Parley! Ah, your rudimentary diplomatic French.

(The Little Tramp mimes himself miming.)

SECRET BEAUTY: Quite the metanarrative dance, friend.
(*beat, to the King*)
I know that communication has taken place. The lighthouse had flared to life; I followed the glow of the light. The Little Tramp here was dancing with one of the skeletons, then set them to bow before him.

THE KING: A coup, was it?

(The Little Tramp holds out his palms and frantically shakes his head, then kneels and begs for mercy. He points to the King, then to himself, then gestures suggesting trading derby for crown and back again.)

FRENCHMAN: California!

BOMBSHELL: Hollywood?

FRENCHMAN: No. I believe we are farther north.

BOMBSHELL: How do you know?

FRENCHMAN: The politics of the moment. Technologically overdetermination, the potentate fearing the subaltern, utopian architecture that has fallen to shit, and I personally cannot stand it here.

SECRET BEAUTY: Makes sense.

THE KING: What did these beings want, niece?

FRENCHMAN: I'd imagine they want for nothing.

SECRET BEAUTY: Close. They want for *nothingness.*

FRENCHMAN: Ah, but it is beyond their power to extinguish their selves. They have fallen into despair.

BOMBSHELL: Do we have the power to extinguish ourselves, egghead?

FRENCHMAN: Egghead!

BOMBSHELL: Would you prefer frog-face, buster?

(The Bombshell stomps up to the Frenchman and pokes him in the chest. The Little Tramp follows behind her, his dukes up, ready to defend her.)

FRENCHMAN: There is but one way to find out if we do, mademoiselle. But tell me, do you feel the compulsion to try it? I suspect that you do not. Even *I* do not. But this island's previous inhabitants must have at one point been contemplating their own ends but found themselves unable to achieve them. We must imagine Sisyphus unhappy, more profoundly unhappy than anyone else could ever imagine. Life imprisonment is worse than a death sentence when death is forever held at bay by something other than one's own will.

BOMBSHELL: All this philosophy is giving me a headache.

FRENCHMAN: The absurdity of life will do that.

SECRET BEAUTY: Speaking of absurd...

THE KING: Yes?

SECRET BEAUTY: Uh... Do any of you remember what we were doing immediately before the Little Tramp plucked us out of the television?

(The Little Tramp nods in the affirmative, but the other three shake their heads. All four other characters turn to the Little Tramp and wait expectantly. He nods more rigorously, pointing at his temple.)

BOMBSHELL: Well, spit it out!

LITTLE TRAMP: I...uhm...I was here. I was here first. I had a job in a factory. It was going pretty well. I was only yelled at once or twice. Anyway, then I fell down a chute and was chewed up by a massive complex of gears, and then I found myself being chased around in the generator room. There was a big screen on the wall. It started glowing and I jumped in.

FRENCHMAN: You just dressed like that for a proletarian job? How did you keep your hat on?

SECRET BEAUTY: No, the clothes changed! Happened to me too. I was in computer class in school. We have brand new Apple IIs and I was chatting with this really hot transfer student. He didn't know it was me. He sent over a picture and while it was loading I leaned in to see his...uhm...

BOMBSHELL: That's right!

SECRET BEAUTY: And I fell into the screen and was here.

BOMBSHELL: Same with me! I was shooting a musical number for a television variety show. *In color!* Between takes I went to watch the playback on the monitor to make sure my décolletage wasn't too shiny, I tripped on my hem, and then my Charlie saved me with his cane.

FRENCHMAN: I was in the cinema, first row of an otherwise empty theater. I was watching the Little Tramp's film, and saw him go through the screen, thought I'd never seen anything like that before. I stood up, shocked, yawped at the projectionist, and when I turned around again a great hook was reaching for me.

LITTLE TRAMP: I was...lonely. And confused. To be surrounded by color instead of rich blacks and endless grays, to be nearly as thick as I am tall.

BOMBSHELL: I fell in love the moment I laid eyes on you! How could I not? But what's love without an audience to eat their hearts out?

(The Little Tramp sticks out his tongue at the Frenchman.)

FRENCHMAN: Perhaps I too experienced a burst of love at first sight, like a bayonet to the belly on the barricades. Perhaps it is that case that—
(*turns his gaze to the Secret Beauty*)
all of us did.

SECRET BEAUTY: (*ignoring the Frenchman*) How about you, my Lord?

(The King retrieves the horse's head from the ground and holds it to his eye level.)

THE KING: I was...not the monarch of so great a land. Nary a tree in the wood, just like here. Industrial buildings rather than great halls and hearths, the smell of rendered—

SECRET BEAUTY: Fast food mascot king of some sort, gotcha.

THE KING: (*chagrined*) The screen was my own. A court jester with a hamburger for a hat wheeled it to my side so that I could turn it on and show useless eaters what to eat. I glanced at the screen and found myself here. I thought I was being dragged to heaven, for I was already a subject of hell.
(*beat*)
This must be some mistake. All of it. Are you not my niece? And you, are you not my daughter? Am I truly not a king?

FRENCHMAN: It's an old question. Does essence precede existence, or does existence precede essence? But a newer question presents itself--now that we are here, what do we do with ourselves?

THE KING: I'm more interested in the horse costume!

BOMBSHELL: Oh, Daddy. But...yeah!
(*to the Little Tramp*)
How'd you end up such a horse's ass?

SECRET BEAUTY: If you must know...

(The Secret Beauty takes the horse's head from the King and places it over her own head.)

SECRET BEAUTY: I have no wish to marry. So when you, Lord, sent me and my cousin to make a wedding outfit from the meager bounty of the land...

(The Secret Beauty takes the Bombshell's hand and they make a show of skipping about gleefully.)

SECRET BEAUTY: I used one of the martial arts moves that all mousy teenage girls know, and—

(The Secret Beauty clasps both hands on the Bombshell's wrist, and wrings her arm, flipping the Bombshell head over heels.)

BOMBSHELL: Yow! Not very ladylike! Not this time either!

SECRET BEAUTY: Once free, I ran off toward the lighthouse. I figured I could climb it and use the high vantage point to get the lay of the land. I hate the suburbs. I dream of heading to the big city and going to college, of starting a career in the arts, of meeting a guy who wears black turtlenecks and chunky glasses.

(The Frenchman throws up his arms, upset.)

SECRET BEAUTY: I beat Charlie to the lighthouse. I had a goal; he was just waddle-wandering around. There is technology in the lighthouse, stuff more advanced than anything I'd ever seen, but dare I say not more advanced than whatever it is we are.

THE KING: We are?

SECRET BEAUTY: Remember the flowers Charlie picked? They're still around here somewhere, aren't they?

(The Bombshell, still on the ground, thrusts up a hand, holding the remaining flowers.)

SECRET BEAUTY: See. They're burnt. We're light and sound, projections. It's a good thing these islands are barren wastes. We'd start a fire with every step we took if there were still grasses here. Something turned on a machine that had been idle for a very long time. It is intelligent. It knows English.
(*gestures toward the sky*)
It could even interpret gestures and win a game of charades. Well, either that or it is the thing feeding us our thoughts, plotting our moves. We're not even mere players; we're just roles.

FRENCHMAN: (*passionate*) No! I refuse to believe it, though I need not refuse that which is false. We are intelligent beings, moral actors. We give our own lives meaning in the face of meaninglessness. Look at our King. Is he truly an aristo, or is he just a clown for the bourgeoisie? Or worse, a trained ape dressed as royalty to signify nothing but speed and hunger, grease and greed, the oinking of a million pigs?

SECRET BEAUTY: Well...

THE KING: Have a care, sir. Your diplomatic tendencies are fading, and your anarchism is showing, like a rash does, so do nothing and say nothing rash!

FRENCHMAN: Your costume is little better, save for the late addition of the horse's head. And look at Charlie; a gentleman rolled in the dirt until his class origins are obscured. And the princess--does anyone such as her even exist outside of the cinema? The movies taught her how to act; she did not learn to act to produce cinema.

BOMBSHELL: (*climbing to her feet*) Buster, I've had about enough out of you. Charlie, you hold him while I hit him. We'll take turns.

FRENCHMAN: No, listen! You need not be who you are. You can change. We are all damned to be free. Behold!

(The Frenchman removes the horse's head from the Secret Beauty. Her visor and glasses both get stuck in the horse's head. Her hair cascades down her shoulders, and she tilts her head in a certain way, coquettish.)

BOMBSHELL: Whoa! You're hot stuff after all, toots!

THE KING: You are cousins, after all.

FRENCHMAN: You see! You chose to obscure your exterior beauty, so that only the most discerning and mature of men could sense it in you. You chose to—

(The Secret Beauty puts a finger to the Frenchman's lips, not in any erotic way, but just to shut him up.)

SECRET BEAUTY: I can't see without my glasses. Could someone please fish them out of the horse's head. I need my hair up for work. What is wrong with you people?

(The Little Tramp finds the glasses and offers them to the Secret Beauty, but the Frenchman intercepts them.)

FRENCHMAN: Girl. Did you not just tell us that we are phantasms, projections. Our touch sets things in this world smoldering, and we cannot touch one another. Do you even truly *have* eyes?

BOMBSHELL: I still want to know about the horse costume!

THE KING: *Rocinante!* From the famed novel.

LITTLE TRAMP: I...looked up into the light as it shone down on me. I saw a pair of silhouettes; one I think was a man, stooped over with age, the other a girl-child.

SECRET BEAUTY: I saw them too. *With* my glasses on. I had just begun climbing the steps of the lighthouse when the light in the tower turned on. I saw two pairs of feet peeking out from under a great ball of light.

LITTLE TRAMP: The light swung over me and I was gone.

SECRET BEAUTY: Same.

THE KING: And you found yourself...in a novel?

SECRET BEAUTY: In a situation, anyway. A black box room with a high ceiling and a dozen lights, a man in rusty armor and a little pot-bellied fellow next to him.

BOMBSHELL: A theater! Was there an audience?

LITTLE TRAMP: There weren't even seats to be rented out for the price of a ticket. There were no wings, no exit. It was as though the room had been built up around the pair, and somehow around us.

SECRET BEAUTY: We didn't know our lines.

FRENCHMAN: The horse had lines in this?

LITTLE TRAMP: Well for my part I did not.

FRENCHMAN: For the best, horse's ass.

SECRET BEAUTY: When I saw your hand beckoning out of the corner of my eye, from where the black was blackest, cousin, I had to take it.

THE KING: Prepare yourselves, all of you. We shall tilt against the lighthouse!

(BLACKOUT)

SCENE FOUR

The Lighthouse and Beyond

(Near the lighthouse, the exoskeletons are where the LITTLE TRAMP left them, though more PINK GOO has spread upon the stage.)

(THE KING has taken point, with the FRENCHMAN and the SECRET BEAUTY on his left, the FRENCHMAN guiding her with his hand as she is still without her glasses. Immediately behind the KING is the BOMBSHELL, who is carrying the horse costume. THE LITTLE TRAMP is poking around in the pile of refuse.)

BOMBSHELL: Father. Daddy. My King? This is madness, you know. Crazy. Bonkers.

THE KING: What is the worst that could happen to us, my dear.

SECRET BEAUTY: We could be trapped in a small black box forever.

FRENCHMAN: You might say we, all of us, are always trapped in a small black box, and at death all that changes is that we exchange it for a smaller box.

BOMBSHELL: You've been selling that egghead bunk all night.

LITTLE TRAMP: (*holding up a long metal rod he has found*) Aha! Will this do?

THE KING: Yes, it should.

FRENCHMAN: (*peering down at the exoskeletons*) What were you doing with these...men?

SECRET BEAUTY: How do you know they are men?

FRENCHMAN: How did I know you would make the point of asking such a question?

(The Little Tramp walks the rod, which is smoldering in his holographic field hands, over to the King, pointedly ignoring the conversation as he passes, and presents the rod to the King across open palms like a medieval figure.)

BOMBSHELL: But why, Father? Charlie, why?

THE KING: Events such as these must end with either a wedding or a funeral. Get your cousin back in the horse.

FRENCHMAN: No!

THE KING: (*grasping the rod, it smolders in his hands*) The time for debate is over. I will charge against this giant.

FRENCHMAN: You don't need to harm her. You know the horse is but your niece and your daughter's lover—

THE KING: Lover!

FRENCHMAN: In a suit. You know that pipe in your hand is no lance, and the lighthouse is neither giant nor windmill.

SECRET BEAUTY: It hasn't been a functional lighthouse in thousands of years. Yet it hasn't collapsed into ruin.

(The gazes of all five people turn toward the exoskeletons.)

SECRET BEAUTY: I suppose that for a long time there was a society to maintain it, or a repair crew that fell to ruin first.

FRENCHMAN: Your daughter is right, Your Majesty, this is absurd.

THE KING: Then you should agree that I must do it.

FRENCHMAN: (*clutching the Secret Beauty*) But she must not!
(*beat, stands tall*)
I'll take her place.

THE KING: Perhaps you should take the Little Tramp's place.

(The Little Tramp climbs back upon the pile of garbage and whistles and waves his hat at the lighthouse. As he stands atop the pile, it settles a bit, leading to a bit more goo oozing out from between pieces of refuse.)

(The lighthouse flares to life, and a pair of figures, their features obscured by being backlit, stand in front of the light. Their height and bearing are suggestive of PROSPERO and MIRANDA.)

BOMBSHELL: (*looking up*) They're up there.

THE KING: Take courage, Daughter.
(*beat*)
My steed!

(The Frenchman takes the horse's head from the Bombshell and places it over his own head.)

SECRET BEAUTY: What are you doing?

FRENCHMAN: Sparing you. You'll not be able to charge with the King on your back, and without your glasses.

SECRET BEAUTY: You could give them back.

FRENCHMAN: This is one reason why I do not.

SECRET BEAUTY: What are the others?

FRENCHMAN: You are beautiful and I love you.
Marry me.

COLLECTIVE VOICE: A wedding!

(Everyone stops, startled, though the Little Tramp and the Secret Beauty are somewhat less surprised.)

THE KING: (*shouting up at the lighthouse*) Or a funeral! Your own. You have exiled us to his desolate land, a land you've brought to ruin and despair.

FRENCHMAN: Surely despair is the natural state of this place. There's not even a sea to stare out over for solace.

COLLECTIVE VOICE: The waters boiled away long ago. At first slowly, and then all at once. All we could do was watch.

FRENCHMAN: Cursed with immortality rather than freedom, is it?

THE KING: We'll see how cursed with immortality they are. Bend down so I might straddle your shoulders.

BOMBSHELL: (*to the Little Tramp*) Any bright ideas, hot stuff?

(The Little Tramp takes the Bombshell in his arms, dips her as he did the exoskeleton and kisses her deeply, but a HUGE ELECTRONIC SOUND rings out, and the pair fly away from one another. They rise, rubbing their faces and lips, as if recovering from a painful shock.)

BOMBSHELL: (*in pain*) Ugh! That was not the lay-one-on-me I wanted laid on me!

(The Little Tramp wobbles about, still recovering from the shock, then sits down on the ground, defeated. The Frenchman sinks to one knee and allows the King to mount his shoulders. The Secret Beauty kneels as well, but to peer at the exoskeleton—she needs to look closely as she is without her glasses. She takes the skull cap off one of the exoskeletons and puts it on her own head, and then does the same with the face plate.)

COLLECTIVE VOICE: Two weddings!

THE KING: Charge!

(With a grunt, the Frenchman charges, with the King on his back, toward the lighthouse. The lighthouse's great lamp flares to life, shooting a blinding light at the pair. Thanks to the horse's head, the Frenchman is not dazzled, but the King is. He throws up his hands, drops his ersatz lamp, and tumbles off his mount. The Frenchman falls after him and lands on top of him.)

COLLECTIVE VOICE: Beings of light, blinded by light. You've convinced yourselves that you are something you are not.

THE KING: I do not require the criticism of lighthouse keepers *or* philosophers!

(The Frenchman pulls himself free of the horse's head. The Bombshell rushes to comfort her father, the Little Tramp following close behind. The Secret Beauty is now fully encased in an exoskeleton. The light grows more intense, flooding the entire stage, making clear that the island is only a set and revealing the rigging and catwalks of the stage.)

BOMBSHELL: Get out of the spotlight!

LITTLE TRAMP: Don't look at it!

(Of course the Frenchman, being contrary, turns his face toward the light. The beam tightens and focuses on him, plunging the rest of the stage into darkness. He shivers and shakes and folds into himself. The Secret Beauty wades into the light, protected by the exoskeleton, grabs one of the Frenchman's limbs, and drags him out of the light beam. The lighthouse lamp is extinguished, and the lighting on stage returns to normal. Prospero and Miranda are revealed as also being primarily exoskeletal, though some traces of flesh and bits of ragged clothing hang from their largely metallic forms.)

FRENCHMAN: My love! Thank you!

THE KING: (*standing*) What happened? Did we win?

COLLECTIVE VOICE: You.

(The lighthouse lamp shines again, but less intensely, illuminating the Secret Beauty in her new body.)

COLLECTIVE VOICE: How does it feel? To have a physical body?

FRENCHMAN: (*pressing his hand against the Secret Beauty's breastplate*) No smoldering, no heat.

BOMBSHELL: Darn, toots. Announcing "No smoldering" is no way to woo a woman, much less my beautiful first cousin.

COLLECTIVE VOICE: We must apologize. All of this was an accident. The quaint device that powered these islands, and powered these forms, has long since powered down. A solar flare blanketed the hemisphere with radiation. Even we could barely hang on to a flicker of life. A random power surge momentarily recharged a narrative generation device and led to you all manifesting as beings of light and shadow.

LITTLE TRAMP: Oh? And what are you then? Not flesh and bone.

COLLECTIVE VOICE: Not anymore. There hasn't been a man of flesh and bone born in this world for one thousand years.

THE KING: Now, listen here, clockwork couple. Come down from your perch and fight like men! This kingdom shall be ours.

FRENCHMAN: Ours?

(The Secret Beauty hands the Frenchman a faceplate liberated from one of the other exoskeletons.)

SECRET BEAUTY: Don't speak.
(*she holds the faceplate over his face*)
Don't speak.

(They kiss. For real.)

(The Little Tramp and the Bombshell look at one another. There is only one complete exoskeleton left on the ground.)

LITTLE TRAMP: Oh. I'm sorry.

BOMBSHELL: Don't be.

COLLECTIVE VOICE: We are sorry. So much has been lost over these past millennia. We have only palimpsests and recycled files, pirate copies and scanlations, content analyses and unlucky guesses, script-kiddies and quaint devices. If there's a play, it's been lost; if there is a novel, its translation is traitorous; if there are collaborators, they've been shot; and if there's a language, the machines are still learning it... but with nobody—and no bodies—with which to check their work.

(The Bombshell walks over to her father and whispers in his ear at length. While she does so, the Frenchman quickly slips out of his long coat and starts sealing himself within the exoskeleton. With every piece attached, the audience hears a metallic click. The Little Tramp walks over to the last exoskeleton, takes off his coat and hat, attaches the skullcap and faceplate of the last exoskeleton to himself, replaces the derby on top of his new metal head, and continues to outfit himself.)

THE KING: Yes, dear. You are correct. Clever! Genius! As wise as you are docile and sweet.
(*shouted up to Prospero and Miranda*)
Hear this! Two weddings, five funerals, seven beings in search of a life beyond the confines of the stage.

(The three exoskeletons, now re-empowered by the holographic characters, take positions behind the King and peer up at the lighthouse, where the two dying exoskeletons are silent, and unmoving.)

THE KING: Or as someone put it once, deposited in some memory bank like a golden coin to be spent only now, "Love and War are the same thing, and stratagems and policy are as allowable in the one as in the other." (*holding out his arms*) Come down here and let us embrace.

COLLECTIVE VOICE: (*after a long moment*) You two come up here.

(With whoops of joy, the King and the Bombshell rush up to the door and step through it.)

(LIGHTS OUT.)

(LIGHTS BACK UP.)

(The sets are down. Five exoskeletons in a black box take an extravagant series of bows to pre-recorded crowd noises from an audience much larger than any room in which this play is to be performed. Actual audience applause and cheers during performances of this play are strictly prohibited.)

Acknowledgments

This one was a long time coming, and I kept the manuscript mostly to myself. The idea was inspired by the 2019 essay "Caliban Never Belonged to Shakespeare" by Marcos Gonzalez in *LitHub*, which reminded me of my own childhood as a member of an immigrant family who rented Paul Mazursky's *Tempest* on VHS because it took place in Greece, and there was Raúl Juliá wearing the same sleeveless t-shirt and big mustache all the male relatives in my family had, speaking with a passable Greek accent, as "Kalibanos." So I acknowledge Gonzalez, Juliá, and the great and brief culture of mom-and-pop video stores of New York City.

2019 was a low point for me, but I did enjoy my retail job at Books Inc., Berkeley, though it paid minimum wage. Another spark—what sort of book would I like to shelve in the store as I worked to sell the books of my more successful author friends? Something slim and fun and connected to the so-called canon, but also a détournement. Wouldn't you know it, but then a shipment of the 2017 reissue of *Mrs. Caliban* by Rachel Ingalls was in the very next box of books I had to open. So thank you to the store and the staff! and Ingalls.

Then came COVID and isolation, just like Caliban/Kalivas faced, and my friends Molly Tanzer and Seth Cully did much to lift my spirits via the power of online chat. Molly and Seth, I acknowledge you! (Picture me pointing one finger to the sky.) Also during isolation, Cara Hoffman invited me to join *The Anarchist Review of Books*, which gave me something to do, so thank you to her and the rest of the collective, particularly D. G. Gerard. And of course, I must acknowledge the work of Peter Greenaway and Michael Nyman, whose vision for *Prospero's Books* has been an inspiration for decades.

About the Author

Nick Mamatas is the author of several novels, including the instant cult classic *Move Under Ground* and the speculative thriller *The Second Shooter*. His short fiction has appeared in *McSweeney's*, *Best American Mystery Stories*, Tor.com, and many other venues. Nick is also an anthologist; his latest is *120 Murders: Dark Fiction Inspired by the Alternative Era*. Nick's fiction and editorial work has been nominated for the Hugo, World Fantasy, Locus, and Bram Stoker Awards. He is also a member of the editorial collective of *The Anarchist Review of Books*.

Also by CLASH Books

STRANGE STONES

Mary SanGiovanni & Edward Lee

THE MAN WHO SAW SECONDS

Alexander Boldizar

THE KING OF VIDEO POKER

Paolo Iacovelli

THE RACHEL CONDITION

Nicholas Rombes

BAD FOUNDATIONS

Brian Allan Carr

KILL THE RICH

Jack Allison & Kate Shapiro

THE LAST NIGHT TO KILL NAZIS

David Agranoff

CATHERINE THE GHOST

Kathe Koja

THE QUEEN OF SATURN AND THE PRINCE IN EXILE

Errick Nunnally

www.ingramcontent.com/pod-product-compliance
Lightning Source LLC
Jackson TN
JSHW021908160825
89473JS00004B/5

9781960988799